A Cold Love After All

Tyanna

BRINGING LIFE TO URBAN FICTION

Frost Bite: A Cold Love After All

Copyright © 2021 by Tyanna

Published by Tyanna Presents

www.tyannapresents1@gmail.com

Synopsis

After a lifetime of abuse from her mother, seventeen-year-old January McQueen is placed in foster care with a family that seems loving... on the surface. January finally feels at home, making friends with her foster siblings and doing all the things a normal teenaged girl would do. Then, she meets her foster mother's son, Dahmere Frost. No matter how much January was feeling him, Frost paid her no attention. She holds on to the hope that one day, he'll notice her.

Twenty-year-old Frost is finally home after doing a two-year bid. Up to his old tricks, his main focus was getting back to the streets and slinging more dope than before. Sure, he notices the little cutie that his mother is fostering, but she's too young, and he has no time for women right now.

January is victimized again, this time by her foster father, a trauma that sends her running to the streets. Desperate and alone, she's willing to do anything to survive, a choice that takes her into some dark and dangerous places.

One night, Frost comes to her rescue, and January realizes all the feelings she'd had are still there. Will Frost finally admit to their mutual attraction, or will January's feelings stay one-sided?

ONE

January

Every day at 3 PM, when the bell rang while I was in my last period class, for some reason, I got excited. It was like I was almost to the finish line. It meant I was a step closer to graduation day, and my eighteenth birthday. All I wanted was out of Tracy McQueen's house. I had endured so much pain while living underneath her roof, and I just couldn't wait 'til I got out of there. I was supposed to move in with my granny, but she passed away right before the paperwork was cleared. I didn't wanna go to a foster home because you never knew who you were moving in with, so I figured I would just stay there and deal with this bullshit.

I tried not to have friends because I would never want them to know what was going on in my household, so I just decided to be a loner. The most excitement I had was my school papers and projects. I was what you would called a nerd, but I was a fine one. I didn't get teased like most nerds did because Tracy kept me dressed in the finer things, but trust me, it came with a price.

Walking up to my home, I noticed a car parked out in front that didn't look familiar, which meant Tracy was probably in there on good bullshit, and I wasn't in the mood. I had two tests today, and a paper to study for. All I wanted to do was shower and get some studying done. Once I opened the door, moans could be heard from the living room area. Not trying to look at what was going on, I tried to hurry up and walk by to head straight to my room. But I felt someone staring at me, and when I looked up, we were eye to eye with each other until I turned away.

I looked to the side of him, and Tracy was bent over the couch, while an older man hit it from the back, and ole' boy that was looking at me was sitting in the chair next to them—just watching while stroking his diseased peter. Trying to get the sight before me out of my head, I hurried and ran to my room, then shut the door. Once I got in my room, I threw my things on the bed and sat down. The tears started to run down my face, and I just didn't understand why my mama was like this.

She claimed after my daddy left her, when I was first born, she's had no choice but to use what she got to get what she wanted. When I was younger, I believed her, but as I started to get older, I realized that there were other things she could have done to make money. But all she wanted to do was sell pussy. And ever since I turned fourteen, she sold mine as well. It was like niggas paid top dollar for me since I was so young. The sound of banging on my room door brought me out of my thoughts. Kind of scared, but knowing I didn't have a choice, I opened my room door, and the dude that I came into eye contact with was standing there.

"Cookie, get cleaned up, baby! You have a job to do!" my mama yelled from the living room, calling me by my childhood nickname.

The dude stood there smiling once he heard her say that. I tried to close the door, but he placed his foot in the way.

"Can you move so I can get cleaned up?"

"No. I wanna watch you get cleaned up. I'm paying my money, so we do this my way, little girl."

Not paying him any mind, I tried to close the door, but I wasn't strong enough. He used his force to push the door open, then he smacked me across my face, causing me to fly to the floor. Once he was in, he closed the door behind him. He walked over to me and snatched me up off the floor, then threw me on the bed. Once I was on the bed, I looked to my side to see what I had on my nightstand to hit him with. There was nothing but a journal and pen sitting on top of it.

"You're such a pretty girl. All you have to do is cooperate if you don't want to get hurt," he said while smiling at me again.

While looking at me with lustful eyes, he unzipped his pants, then pulled his dick out. It was, indeed, a nice size, but he had all types of white pus bumps on it, and I swear, on my dead granny, this nigga was not sticking that in me. Thinking fast, I grabbed the pen off my journal and stabbed it right in his neck, causing all his blood to shoot out on me. The way that blood splattered I knew this wasn't going to end well. I knew right then and there I must have killed this asshole.

I hurried and slid the body off me, jumped up, and headed towards the front door. When I went past the living room, Tracy was still in the act, but when she saw me run, she stopped and started screaming my name. I hurried and got out of the door and knocked on my neighbor's door. Once the door opened, she looked at me with wide eyes and hurried to pull me in.

"OH MY GOD! Baby, are you ok?"

"He tried to rape me…he tried to rape me," I cried while she held me.

Ms. Johnson always had a feeling something was going on in my home, but I would always tell her I was good. I didn't wanna go to foster care, but I knew this incident was surely sending me there, unless he was dead, and I was going down for murder.

"Shhhh…baby, you're good here with me. I have to call the police, January."

I didn't say anything. I just nodded my head *ok*. I knew what the outcome of this would be, but at this point, I needed a change. I needed to get away from Tracy. She was a sick individual, and I had been going through this since I was fourteen. Four years of men touching me, me performing sexual acts, and sometimes, Tracy touching me to please the men. I was sick, and I was tired, and shouldn't no one ever have to feel like a prisoner/sex slave in their own home. Especially a teenager.

＊＊＊＊＊＊

Three months later…

I had spent three long months in a group home. After they had found out all the things my Mama had going on, they locked her ass up. Come to find out, this nasty bitch had videos in the house that she must have been using to get off when she was home alone. I had been doing well and was getting counseling. I was even caught up with my schoolwork. Considering all I've been through, my caseworker said she admired me because I've been holding up and was still handling my business in school. Though, I went through my depression stages, I still knew what I had to do if I wanted to live better than what my childhood was.

"McQueen!" one of the counselors came to my room, calling me by my last name.

My caseworker had called a week ago and said they found me placement. Since I still had about six months to go until my eighteenth birthday, and five months until graduation, I had to be placed in a foster home until then. I had no other family, so this is what had to be done. I grabbed my belongings and made my way to the door. The counselor walked me to the front desk, and there my caseworker was: Ms. Ebony Lucas. She was so beautiful, kind of putting me in mind of Tika Sumpter.

"Hey, January! You ready to go?" Ms. Lucas asked.

"Yes, I'm ready." I smiled, but on the inside, I was nervous and scared.

Going to a foster home had always been a fear of mine because you never know if you're going with good people or monsters, but it was nothing I could do. I had no choice.

"I know you're nervous, but just think—six more months to go—seven at the most. Then, you can go on your own, as long as you can afford to. I told you once you graduate with good grades, I'll help as much as I can," Ms. Lucas assured me.

They weren't supposed to help, but she promised me she would, and I believed her. After she got finished signing paperwork, we made it out of the door and into her car. Today was a start of a life-change for me. I just hoped that it was a good one because I didn't know if I would be able to deal with any more pain in my life.

TWO

Dahmere (Frost)

It was finally January 1, 2021, and I was walking out of the Camden County Correctional Facility. When I got shipped back here two months ago, I knew my time was almost up. I had been away for two years, and I now have a new outlook on life. Seeing my pops sitting in the car waiting for me, all I could do was shake my head. I couldn't stand his ass, but I signed my soul to the devil years ago. Now I was stuck working for him until I figured my life out. Once I walked up to the car, he hopped out and pulled me in for a one-arm hug.

"Hey, my boy! I'm glad to see you make it out of there." He smiled while patting me on top of my head like he did when I was younger.

"Come on, Dalton, with all that dumb shit." I scoffed, growing annoyed.

He didn't say shit. He just walked back to the driver's side of the whip and hopped in.

Once I got in the car, he looked at me, and I knew he was about to say some bullshit. "What's up?" I asked, now facing him.

"I got some good news and some bad."

"Cough that shit up."

"Money has been low, so I couldn't get you a place. So, I had to get you paroled to your mama's crib."

I looked at him as if he had two fucking heads. "Man, listen. You gon' have to fix that shit. You know damn well I ain't supposed to be in the house with them kids," I snapped.

My mama ran a foster home, and my pops knew this shit was wrong on every level, but as always, he was able to finesse the law and get shit done his way. Which is why I never really spent time in jail, but this last time, I spent two fucking years behind bars. Reason why I was giving him attitude. He got me out here pushing his shit, and his name stayed clean. I ain't no fucking minor, and I ain't trying to fuck up my record any longer. From here on out, I'm trying to work towards getting my shit straight.

"You gon' be alright, son. I got some shit done whereas though it'll be alright for you to stay there for a couple of months. I also got some work that I have for you and my young boy that took over while you were down. We did a raid the other day and in got some product."

"Do you even know who shit you stole?"

"Why? Did that ever matter before?" he asked.

"Look, Pops. I ain't trying to be moving like we were before I went in. We need a better system. I can't afford to get caught up again. You're a fucking cop with so much power. You need to make sure I'm good. I wasn't supposed to do two fucking years, Dalton. So, I don't know what you need to do, but if you want me to continue to sling ya shit, we work the way I wanna do this. I'll meet up with you and your youngin' to see what the fuck y'all talking about, but it has to be my way or no way. And get me an apartment. I don't wanna be in my mama house longer than a month."

I knew he didn't like how I talked to him, but I also knew I was all he had that he could trust. Yeah, he dealt with a new cat, but I knew Dalton, and I knew damn well he didn't really know this dude.

"I'm sorry you had to do time, but you home—you have no bracelet, and you only have to meet with the PO once a week for a couple of months. Now let's get you to your mama's crib. I got you two phones: one for personal, and one for business. I also had LaVonya go shopping for you, so you should have clothes there."

The thought of my little sister caused a smile to creep up on my face. I missed her little spoiled ass so much, and I was proud that she was now in twelfth grade with five months to go. I gave him a head nod, letting him know I heard him. He then peeled off and headed to my mama's crib.

After throwing his sirens on and speeding and dodging through traffic, we made it to my mama's house. And she had the nerve to have a *Welcome Home* banner out front. I wasn't off this, but I knew her and Vonnie missed me, so I decided to put a smile on my face to act like I was happy about it. The minute I exited the car and walked in the house, everyone screamed, "Welcome home, Frost!" I wasn't even gon' lie. I wasn't really into this, but seeing faces I ain't seen in two years had a smile on a nigga's face.

"Hey there, baby!" My mama walked up to me and pulled me in for a hug.

Then Vonnie came up behind me. "Hey, big bro! Welcome home."

I looked at my sister, and she was so beautiful. I knew I was going to have to keep the niggas out of her face. "Hey, sis! What's up, beautiful?" I said while pulling her in for a hug.

While I was holding my sister, I felt someone staring at me. I looked up, and it was a chocolate cutie standing over in the corner like she was lost. She must have been one of Vonnie's friends, so I didn't say anything. I just smiled at her and kept hugging my family.

"Come on, baby. Let me fix you a plate, then you can go shower and head out," my mama said, knowing exactly what was about to go down.

I placed my bag under the table, then sat down and waited for her to bring me my plate. I was going to eat, get dressed, and go find some pussy. A nigga was in need due to being away for two years.

******

"Damn, girl, suck that shit!"

I started to feel my dick in the back of this chick name, Eve's, throat. Little mama was some chick I used to fuck with before I got cased. I wasn't really feeling it when I heard she dun' had two kids while I was away. The shit was crazy as fuck. I made sure to ask were they mine, and she told me no, so I just left the shit like that. After she let my shit tickle the back of her throat, she came back up and licked the tip of it like it was a lollipop, before taking it back in her mouth. She then swallowed my shit whole in a swift motion, causing my body to tense up.

I couldn't even hold my composure any longer. My body began to shake, and I shot all my seeds down her throat. Once I was finished shaking, Eve wiped her mouth, then smirked at me, right before taking me back in her mouth once more. After she was done sucking and getting my mans to stand back at attention, she climbed on top of me and slid down on my pole. I let out a moan while biting on my bottom lip.

"Ride, that shit, beautiful! Just like that." I moaned in her ear while she was giving me the ride of my life.

"Fuck…Frost, I missed this dick, baby," she said while starting to move in a fast motion.

Shit, a nigga just got the fuck out of jail. I knew if she kept moving like this, I was going to cum, and I wasn't ready for that. So, I grabbed her waist and slowed her ass down, then I flipped her over and threw her legs on my shoulders. The way she yelled out in pleasure was turning me the fuck on. The more she yelled, the more I started working her with deep, long, slow strokes. I felt her pussy muscles contracting on my dick, and I couldn't hold my nut in any longer.

"You ready to cum with me, beautiful?" I asked in a husky tone while speeding up the pace.

"Yessss, Frost, I'm ready to cum!" she yelled out, causing my body to react, and we both came long and hard.

Once we both was satisfied, we just laid there, cuddled up. I was glad her kids were with her mama because I was tired, and I knew after that sex, my ass was definitely drifting off to sleep.

THREE

Dalton

It had been two days since I'd dropped Frost off, and he has yet to answer any of my phone calls. From the day I picked him up, I wasn't feeling his attitude. I don't know what the fuck went down when he was locked up, or who the fuck was putting bullshit in his head. But I wasn't feeling it. I had been there for him since he first got in trouble when he was younger for shoplifting. From that day on, I had him working for me. Wasn't no kid of mine going to be in the system for doing bullshit. If he was going to do anything, he was going to work for me and really get this bread. I know I ain't shit for doing this, but I needed someone I could trust on my team, and what better person could I get besides my seed?

"Are you even sure he's going to show up?" the young boy, Bruce, I had working for me asked.

"I told you he called this morning and said he would be here today."

"I'm just making sure. This nigga been home almost three days, and we still ain't got to business yet. He just did two years. Why the fuck he ain't trying to make this money? I don't have time for no bullshit like this, Big D."

"First of all, the name is Dalton. Stop calling me that Big D shit," I barked.

"And secondly, don't worry about the moves I'm making. My boy, you don't even know me," Frost replied while walking in.

Bruce jumped up and walked over to Frost, and these cats were doing a whole stare-down. I wasn't going to be dealing with no shit like this. We all were trying to make money, and that was exactly what we were fucking doing.

"Come on, man, let's chill," Hassan said while standing in between Bruce and Frost. Hassan aka Haas was Frost's righthand man, and he only moved when Frost moved. I was trying to get him to work for me while Frost was down, but he wouldn't. He only had loyalty to Frost.

"The only reason I'mma let that smart shit go is because I need to make this bread to feed my seeds."

"Nigga, go on and puff ya chest out in somebody else's fucking face. You don't even fucking know me, so don't come starting shit you can't finish. Dalton, what the fuck is this meeting about? I have shit to do, and sitting here arguing with a sucka ass nigga ain't one."

I looked at the both of them with so much fucking anger. This shit was going to go my way, or no way at all.

"I'mma need you two to fucking kiss and make up. We have work to do, and y'all two beefing for no fucking reason ain't it. I can't have neither of you fucking up the money. So, this is what is going to go down. Both of you will be on different parts of the city. I need you both to form your own team and have them pushing the product.

"I need men that are not snitches, and I need men that are hungry. I need men that don't mind getting they hands dirty to get it out the mud. I need determined niggas. Frost, I already know you have a couple of them niggas who wouldn't even fuck with me while you were down, and that is definitely loyalty."

"That's what I've been doing for the past couple of days. I was getting my old crew back together. I just need to make sure you have a better lawyer on standby, weapons, and money for funerals if need be. I just wanna make sure my team is straight while putting their life on the line for us."

I sat and looked at Frost. This dude had really been on some other shit since he got home. I taught him everything about the game. Well, everything I wanted him to know, but it seemed like he's been doing his own homework while locked away.

"I'll make sure I arrange for all of that. First, I'm about to start y'all both off with this. Yo', Louis, bring me them two duffle bags!" I yelled out to my righthand.

When he entered the room, he sat a bag in front of Frost, then one in front of Bruce. After he did that, he made his way back over to Frost and held his hand out for him to shake. Once he got a hold of Frost's hand, he pulled him up out his seat and in for a hug.

"How you been, knuckle head?" Louis asked.

Louis had been both of my kids' Godfather since they were born, and he's been around since we were younger. He kind of reminded me of Hassan and Frost's relationship. The only thing about Louis was, he wasn't a cop. He had his own security detail business that was doing extremely well. He did, of course, help me with the street shit from time to time, but not often. His wife, Latisha, would have a fucking fit if she knew.

"I'm good, Poppy! How about you? How's Ms. Latisha?" Frost asked.

"She's good. You better make your way over there to see her."

"True, indeed. True, indeed. I miss y'all so much. How my God-brothers doing?" Frost asked, referring to Louis' twelve-year-old twin boys.

"They good! I told you bring ya ass over there. That way, you can see everyone. As a matter of fact, I'mma have Tisha cook Sunday, then you and Vonnie can come by."

"Alright, sounds good. I'm there," Frost assured him.

"Okay, now can we get back to business?" I asked, crashing their little family reunion.

Frost just looked at me and shook his head, and Louis did the same. Yeah, I hated their relationship, and I think I did because Frost and I couldn't seem to get shit together. Now as far a LaVonya? She loved me with all her heart. I loved both my kids, but it was something different about my princess that led me to favor her more. Victoria, their mother, would always say Frost and I clashed because he was a younger version of me.

"Nigga, you always on some childish shit. Frost, I'll see you Sunday, and don't forget to tell Vonnie," Louis said while making his way out of the door.

"Now as I was saying. I want y'all to form a team and get this shit sold. Once you're finished, hit me on the business line, then we can set up for you both to get more.

Any shorts or fuck ups, it comes out of your money. So, you better make sure your team is solid."

"Are we finished here?" Frost asked.

"Bruce, I want you to handle all of the Southside, while, Frost, you handle the North and Eastsides. You two should not cross each other's paths unless some beef comes your way. Which shouldn't be a problem. Then, when you need product, you hit the business line. I also would like us to meet up monthly just to go over how things are running. Emergency meetings are only called when there is a fuck up, and I'm hoping we should be able to get this money without any of them. Do we have an understanding?" I asked while looking at them both.

Once they both gave me a head nod, I signaled for them both to get the fuck out of my face. I'm hoping this shit goes the way I planned. I would hate for them two to kill each other. After everyone left, since I was on the graveyard shift tonight, I made a call to my ex to let her know to meet me at our spot. I had a couple hours to spare, and I needed to lay up real quick. I wanted my ex, nobody else. I just hoped she could get away from her husband.

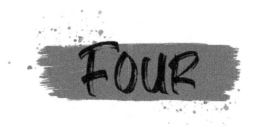

FOUR

LaVonya (Vonnie)

I hated school with a passion and couldn't wait 'til this shit was over. I was sitting in the back of Mrs. Charles' class and didn't understand shit about this assignment. I definitely needed a tutor but was kind of embarrassed to ask about one. What the fuck would Vonnie, the most popular girl in school, need with a damn tutor?

"Okay, class, time is up. If you didn't finish it, you'll need to get it done with tonight's homework."

I just looked up at her and rolled my eyes. I was never going to get this finished, *and* my homework too. The bell rang, and it was time for first lunch. Of course, my lunch was third lunch, but I went to them all. I didn't like my Chemistry class, anyway. The feeling of someone standing next to me brought me out of my thoughts.

"Hey, can you show me where the lunchroom is?" my new foster sister said with her head hanging low.

"Yes, I'll show you, but you have to lift your head up, pooh. You are walking down the hall with me. I can't be walking around with someone that looks like she feels sorry for herself. Hold your head up, girl. You fine as hell with a body to die for."

I wasn't lying. January McQueen was beautiful. We were the same age, and we seemed to dress similar, but you could tell she had some deep shit going on in her life. She was chocolate with ass, hips, and breasts. She dressed nice, so it really was no reason why she should have been holding her head down. That was the reason I knew she was going through shit.

"Thanks for the compliment, but I don't feel sorry for myself. So, you didn't have to say that part," she sassed while rolling her eyes.

I just looked at her, sucked my teeth, and got up to show her where the cafeteria was. Once we made it in the hallway, like always, all the cool kids walked on one side of the hall, and the nerds walked on the other. I noticed all the stares at January and me. I knew no one knew who she was, but they knew she was cool because she was with me.

"Vonnie, what's up, boo?" my girl, Syrah, asked.

"I'm good, pooh! On my way to first-period lunch."

"Ewe...not first-period. You know that shit be corny."

"I'm walking my friend, January, there. She's new here."

"Your friend, hmm…if this is your friend, why don't your best friend know about her?" Syrah asked—in jealous mode—like always.

"Don't start, Sy! Now let's go. I'm hungry."

We made our way to the cafeteria looking like Hollywood, as always. Once we made it in the door, all eyes were on us. We walked over to our original seat with January following behind.

"So, Ms. January, where you from?"

"I'm from around," January sassed.

"What? Did she just get smart with me?" Syrah asked with an attitude.

"Chill out, Sy. She new to this place and still trying to learn everyone."

I could tell right now that Syrah and January were not going to get along at all. I wasn't about to play with these two, though. One has been my friend for years, and the other lived in the same home as me temporarily, so I had to keep it cordial.

"Whatever, Vonnie! Now what y'all think about the test coming up?"

"Y'all already know I'm going to fuck up. I don't wanna get a tutor because I ain't trying to fuck up my reputation."

"Well, if you need one, Vonnie, you should get one," Sy said.

"I'm not doing that, and you know it," I replied.

"How about you pay Clarence ugly ass for the cheat-sheets to the finals? I heard last year he made a killing doing that shit, and everyone that purchased, passed," Sy said.

"Good shit! I forgot all about his ass. I'm gon' check him out before we leave school today."

"You shouldn't do that. You can mess up if someone was to find out," January said.

"No one will find out. This is what we do," Sy assured.

"I just wouldn't chance it. You never know when or if that boy is going to get caught. I can help you if you want me to. It'll just take hard work, dedication, and less partying."

I looked at January and then looked at Syrah. January did have a point, but I didn't wanna agree with her while we were here because I didn't want Syrah to be mad at me.

"No partying?! I don't know about all that. It's my senior year. It's all types of parties going on."

"Aye! That's my BFF!" Syrah said while dancing in her seat, causing January to turn her nose up at her.

These two were going to give me a headache.

We sat around and talked while we ate lunch until Mrs. Foster came and got me for being in the wrong lunch. I was pissed, but I knew she was right. This was twelfth grade, and I didn't need to be fucking up. Being as though I was hanging on by a thread, I needed to get my shit together before I had an unhappy family come graduation day. They all were happy I made it to the twelfth grade and were looking forward to me becoming something.

* * * * * * * *

I was finally finished with afterschool detention for skipping class. I had to go because if I wouldn't have, they would have called my home, and I didn't feel like hearing my mama's mouth. While I walked to the school parking lot to hop in my car, loud music coming from a 2019 Charger could be heard pulling up behind me. I looked up, and this dude was pulling up on the side of me.

"Hey, shawty! Let me holler at you for a second." He was fine as fuck. The chocolate skin, pretty hair, and a full beard was it for me.

"What you wanna holler a me for?" I cooed while batting my eyes.

"You fine as fuck, lil' mama, and I could use someone as fine as you on my arm," he said, sounding corny as fuck, causing me to laugh. "I know that was corny, but I had to say something to make you smile," he said while getting out of the car.

When he got out, I took in his appearance, and it screamed money. I wasn't no gold digger, but I was raised knowing a woman deserved the finer things, and if a dude looked like a bum, he didn't even deserve my conversation.

"It definitely was corny, but you got the smile you wanted out of me. What's your name, and where you from?" I asked, making sure he wasn't where Frost was from.

"My name is Bruce, lil' mama, and I'm from the Southside. What's ya name, and where you from?"

"My name is LaVonya, but everyone calls me Vonnie. That's all you gon' get out of me until we get to know each other." I smiled again, causing him to do the same.

"Oh, so I can get to know you better?" he asked, showing off his pretty white teeth.

"Yup, but only on my terms. Here's my phone. Program your number in, and I'll call you when I'm ready for us to hang out," I said, being truthful.

"On your terms, huh? Just don't make me wait too long, ma. Because I'll be back up here looking for ya little ass."

After he programmed his number in my phone, he walked over to my car and held his hand out for my keys. Then he hit the unlock button and opened the door for me. Once I got in, he handed me the keys, then closed the door.

"I'll talk to you later, sweetheart," he said while hopping in his ride.

"How you know I'mma talk to you later?!" I yelled to him.

"Because I just know, Vonnie." He winked while blasting his music, then peeled off.

I didn't know what it was about him, but I wanted his fine chocolate ass. His swag was everything, and he had my little fresh ass intrigued.

FIVE

January

I was adjusting well to my new living arrangement. Ms. Vickie was so nice, and I really loved her. Vonnie was cool, and so were my little foster brothers, Cash and Cade. They were thirteen. I thought they would be annoying, but nope. Everybody was cool. My older foster brother was Dahmere Frost. He was so fine, and the feeling I experienced whenever I was in his presence was one I'd never felt before. Since I've only been introduced to monsters, and not real men that genuinely weren't perverts, this was different for me. I did feel a little funny around Mr. Luther, which was Ms. Vickie's husband, but I believed it was just me being paranoid because of what I've been through.

"January, I wanted to tell you how proud of you I am. You came here and been showing out, and I just wanted to let you know. When the teacher called me and told me that you only had to go to school half a day because of your academic skills, a huge smile crept upon my face. Then Vonnie told me you went out and got a job. Usually, I wouldn't recommend a job because I don't want it interfering in your schoolwork, but in this situation, you're already doing good. Keep up the good work, baby, and here's a gift from me to you," Ms. Vickie said while walking into the kitchen, where I was sitting doing my homework.

I grabbed the bag from her with a smile on my face. I opened it, and it was a daily planner that had *Black Girl Magic* written across the front. Plus, an iPhone 12 box. I couldn't do shit but get up and run to her with my arms open. When returned the favor, she pulled me in and held me tight. It felt so good. I hadn't been hugged like that since my grandma.

"Thank you so much, Ms. Vickie. I really appreciate this."

"No thanks needed, baby. When you underneath my roof and you're doing good, you get rewarded. Now go ahead and finish up your work, and I'm going to get dinner ready. If I'm going to disturb you, go ahead and head to the back room."

"I'm just about to wrap it up, so I'll be fine. Do you know where Vonnie is?"

"No, I don't, and I've been calling her damn phone. She gon' hear from me today when she gets in here. This the second time this week she didn't answer her phone when I called."

"Oh, ok. We were supposed to have a studying session today. I guess we will do it when she gets in."

"Studying session, huh? Vonnie is about to study? That's good to hear. She always says she ok in school, and her grades be the bare minimum, so I really don't have a reason to complain. But I kind of figured she could use some help because I was sure she could be bringing in better grades than what she's been bringing home. I'm so glad you are helping her," Ms. Vickie cooed.

Ms. Vickie was right. Vonnie could have better grades than this if she would do her damn work. It's like, all she cared about was being cool, and God forbid if she raised her hand to answer a question in class that deemed her as being corny. Or, if she handed in work and got an A. I was so lost with the "being cool and popular" thing. If the shit meant being dumb as hell, I wanted no parts of it. I didn't mind helping her at all. She just needed to be available for the help.

"No problem, Ms. Vickie. I don't mind helping her on my free time."

The sound of someone else entering the kitchen grabbed my attention. I turned to look to see who was entering, and it was Mr. Luther. He walked in, walked straight over to his wife, and pulled her in for a hug, making sure to grab her ass with both his hands.

"Luther, if you don't stop. We have company in here with us."

"Oh, I'm sorry, January. I didn't even see you sitting there. How are you two doing today?" he asked with a huge smile on his face.

"I'm good. Just finishing up my homework."

"I'm good, baby. About to get dinner done before Cash and Cade comes from the Boys and Girls Club."

"Okay. I'm going to the man cave, so you can bring my dinner there when you're finished. January, keep up the great work, as far as school goes. Vickie told me all about it, and I hope you enjoy your gifts," he said while grabbing a water out of the fridge and making his way out of the kitchen.

They seemed like such the perfect couple, but sometimes, things seemed off. It didn't bother me, though, because they were good people to me.

"Thank you, Mr. Luther. I appreciate the both of you for taking me in."

He didn't say anything. He just gave me a head nod, then made his way out of the kitchen.

After I finished up the last of my work, I placed everything into my book bag, then hopped up to see what Ms. Vickie was cooking. She was cutting up chicken breast in small pieces, and I was curious to what she was about to do.

"What you about to cook?"

"Sticky pineapple chicken, white rice, and broccoli."

I have never heard of this, but I wanted to help. "That's different, but it sounds delicious. Do you mind if I help?"

"Of course, not. Go over there and grab an apron off the door."

Ms. Vickie and I talked and enjoyed each other's company while we prepared dinner. I guess staying here until school was finished wouldn't be too bad.

"You're such a pretty girl. All you have to do is cooperate if you don't want to get hurt."

"No, no, no, no...Please, don't hurt me."

I jumped out of my deep slumber, holding my chest and wiping the tears from my eyes. Yeah, I was doing well, but these damn nightmares just wouldn't let up. I sat on the side of the bed, then slid my feet into my furry slides to prepare myself to go downstairs to get something to drink. Once I got downstairs, I walked into the kitchen and grabbed me a mug, then got me a tea bag out of the cabinet. Once I had everything I needed, I made my cup of tea, then made my way into the living room. After scrolling through the TV for about thirty minutes, I noticed one of my favorite movies was on. The minute I saw *Love and Basketball,* a huge smile crept up on my face. It was crazy how much I loved this movie.

The sound of the front door opening brought me out of my thoughts, so I looked towards it, and Frost was walking in. He looked at me and smiled. Not sure if he was looking at me, I turned to look behind me. I wasn't used to him smiling or even saying anything to me, so this was a shock. I knew no one was behind me, but that was how much in shock I was.

"What's good, Miss J?"

"Hey," I said in a low tone.

"What are you doing up this late?"

"I had a nightmare, so I just decided to come down to make me a cup of tea. Since I don't have school tomorrow, I figured I would watch TV until I get tired. Mama Vickie left you a plate in the microwave if you're hungry."

"Alright, cool. Thanks, lil' mama," Frost said, making his way into the kitchen.

The way he just called me lil' mama made butterflies go off in my stomach. He was so damn fine: light skin, big pink lips, a full beard, and not to mention, his dreads were nicely twisted. The fresh line up set everything off.

"What are you watching?" he asked while sitting on the couch next to me, causing me to get nervous.

"*Love and Basketball*," I said in a low tone.

"Do you mind if I watch it with you?"

"No, not at all."

I was supposed to be watching the movie, but I was watching him as well. Every time I felt like he was going to turn to look at me, I hurried and turned my face back to the movie. I didn't wanna look like a creep, but I just couldn't help myself.

Frost was now finished with his food, so he placed his plate on the coffee table, right before he made himself comfortable on the couch, getting closer to me.

"So, where you from, Miss J?"

"I was born and raised in Camden, New Jersey."

"Oh, really? That's crazy because I've never seen you before, as much as I'm in the city."

"My mama didn't let me out much. I was only allowed to come home and go to school. That's it, that's all."

"Oh, ok. I hear you're about to graduate top of your class. That's great. Keeping you in the house was probably the best thing to do, so you wouldn't be out here getting into any trouble."

I thought to myself, *If only he knew what the fuck I went through while being in the house.* "Yeah, I guess," I said in a sad tone.

"You good? Did I say something wrong?"

"No, you're ok."

"So, January is your name. Why did your mama name you that if your birthday is in June?"

"How do you know my birthday? As a matter of fact, how did you know how I was doing in school? You know a lot for someone who has never talked to me before."

"Don't nothing get past me, especially when it's going down in this house."

"Because whoever my deadbeat was, his birthday was in January, and that's how much she was in love with his no-good ass," I snapped, causing him to throw his hands up in the air as if he was surrendering.

"I didn't mean to get you all upset. Let me go ahead and head to bed and leave you alone to watch ya little movie." He chuckled while getting up.

I wanted him to stay, but at the same time, I was tired of all the questions. I just watched him walk away until I couldn't see him anymore. Then I grabbed the throw blanket that always laid across the top of the couch and covered myself up. I continued to watch the rest of the movie until I drifted off to sleep.

SIX

Dahmere (Frost)

Haas and I had shit on lock at all of my traps. Like I had said before, I wanted more than just being one of my pops workers. I wanted to start setting some major goals for my life. I didn't always wanna be in this street shit, and just making money for my pops wasn't cutting it. So, Haas had started a pill flow while I was down, and we had been killing it. The crazy part was, Dalton didn't know shit about it, and what blew my mind was, why didn't he? My pops wasn't up on his shit like he made it seem because if he had shit on lock in the city, why didn't he know what the fuck we had going on? The shit had been going on for a year now.

"Yo', I just picked up money from our favorite white boy," Haas said, entering the trap that I had been in all morning counting my bread.

"That's what's up! Did you give him some product, and did you go get some more scripts from Ms. Trudie?"

"Yup, everything is handled."

"Ok, cool. Hit all the young boys up and let them know this trap will be back up and running tonight—whoever don't mind doing the overnight shift."

"Already done, but yo', the way we doing the shipment is going to have to triple soon. How long do you think we can hide this from your pops? When you were locked down, I only had a limited supply, so we moved slow and in silence. Now we have an unlimited supply, and you had to hire a couple more men to do the drops."

Haas was right. Shit was starting to get big, and I knew word was going to be out soon. I just had to come up with a plan to keep him out of my way. I knew if he found out I was in charge, he would want a big cut, but if I paid someone I trusted to act like it was theirs, maybe he would only want a small portion. Then again, I just didn't know about Dalton these days.

"I know, bro. Just leave that up to me. I'll figure it all out."

No more was said about the situations. Haas and I just continued to count the money so we could give Dalton his part, then deposit the rest in our business account.

The sound of my personal phone vibrating on the table brought me out of my zone. I looked at it and saw it was Vonnie, so I hurried and picked it up.

"Yo', sis, what's up?"

"Hey, big head! I need a favor."

"What might that be?"

"Can you please pick January up from work for me?"

"Why can't you do it?"

"I forgot I had something to do with Sy."

"Ok. What time do she get off?"

"At seven, and I really appreciate this, bro."

"Whatever, Vonnie. Next time you're supposed to do something, you do it. Sy's hoe ass can wait," I snapped, being honest. I didn't care too much for Sy because I knew what type of chick she was. I also knew that Vonnie was her own person, and she'd never let Sy influence her into doing anything.

"OK, bro, dang! I'll make sure next time I'll do it myself."

"Alright, sis. I got shit to do. I'll talk to you later. Be safe, baby girl," I said right before disconnecting our phone call.

"What was that all about?" Haas asked.

"She needs me to pick January up from work at seven."

"How's lil' mama holding up?"

"She's doing good. I think I pissed her off the other night asking her a whole bunch of questions. I was just trying to get to know her since she's staying in my mama crib."

"Nigga, you already know about her, so cut it out." Haas chuckled.

"Fool, you right, but I wanted to see where her head was at. You know them foster kids be having some serious issues."

"So, did you figure out what her story is?"

"No, not yet, but I will soon."

Haas and I busted it up while putting each stack of money where it needed to go. Once we were finished, we loaded our cars with duffle bags. He headed to do a drop. Then I did the same.

****

"We went from rags to riches, uh

Project fences to livin' luxury'

Now we live luxury

Straight out that bottom, nobody gave nothing to

me..."

"Rags2Riches" by Rod Wave blared through my car while I waited for January to come out of the Cherry Hill Mall. I scrolled through my phone looking at all the messages I had from Eve's ass. I wasn't off her lately, but she stayed blowing me up. It had been a minute since I got my dick wet, so I might give her ass a chance tonight.

The sound of Miss J, my nickname for January, knocking on the window brought me out of my thoughts. I hopped out of the car, then walked around to the passenger's side to open it for her. I could tell by the look on her face that she wasn't in the best mood, so I wanted to put a smile on her face. After she was in the car and her seat belt was on, I closed her door, then made my way back around to the driver's side. When I hopped in the car, I looked at her and smiled. She returned the favor with a half-smile.

"You good, ma?"

"Yes, I'm just tired. What happened to Vonnie?"

"She said she had something to do with Sy, so she asked me to grab you. Is that a problem?"

"No, it's not," she said in an annoyed tone.

Knowing that she didn't wanna be bothered, I just kept my mouth shut. I turned the music up loud and made my way to Pennsauken to my mama's crib.

Ten minutes into our ride, she turned the radio down, then turned to look at me. "I'm sorry I'm in a mood today, but it's my G-Moms birthday, and I get like this every year since she's been gone. I really appreciate you taking time out from your busy day to come scoop me."

"You're very welcome. You're like a sister to me, so anything you need, I got you. Just like Vonnie," I assured her while turning my music back up.

Our ride home was continued without either of us saying a word. I understood first-hand how she felt because both of my grandmothers were gone.

SEVEN

LaVonya (Vonnie)

Bruce and I had been kicking it for a couple of weeks now. I had been hiding it from everyone except for Sy. I had to keep my bestie up on game. But I knew for sure I couldn't let my brother and daddy find out. As far as January, I didn't know if I could trust her with my secret. I knew she was sick of me backing out of my tutoring sessions. But Bruce was a busy man, and I had to get up with him when we both had time.

"What you over there thinking about, beautiful?"

"Ummm…nothing," I said while walking over to Bruce and straddling him.

I knew I was being fast, but I also knew I was ready. He made me feel some type of way, and I wanted him so bad. Once I was on top of him, I started kissing all over his neck. While I was kissing on his top part, he was easing out of his bottoms. At that very moment, I was like fuck the foreplay. All I wanted was to feel him inside of me. Once I felt him poking at my entrance, I slid down on his dick.

"Fuck, Bruce!" I yelled out in pleasure while I moved up and down on his pole.

"You good, beautiful?"

"Yessss…I'm good now that I have you inside of me." I moaned out in pleasure.

While I bounced on his erection, he kissed and sucked on my titties. What drove him wild was when I sucked on my own nipple right behind him.

"Damn, ma, I love shit like that." He growled while fucking me back from the bottom.

I felt my nut building up, but I wasn't ready to cum just yet. So, I decided to slow down some.

"You like it slow just like that, baby?" I moaned while I rode him nice and slow.

The way I looked at him must have did something to him because he flipped me over real fast. Then he started kissing my lips passionately right before he began to kiss me down below. After a couple of flicks of his tongue on my clit, I squirmed all over the bed trying to get away from his tongue-lashing.

"Shit, I'm cummin', baby…I'm cummin'!" I yelled out in pleasure.

After I came from his tongue, he slid back inside of me nice and slow. He started moving in and out of me in a fast motion, so I started to tighten my pussy muscles on his erection, causing his eyes to roll back in his head.

"Mmm…Hmm… fuck, ma. I'm about to buss…"

"Me too, Bruce…me too!" I yelled out while my body shook vigorously.

After we both came long and hard, I laid in his arms while we both drifted off to sleep.

The sound of my phone going off caused me to jump out of my deep slumber. I looked at the time, and it was way past my curfew. I could kick myself a hundred times for being late. I knew my mama was going to have a fucking fit. I knew Sy probably covered me, but I also knew my mama wasn't buying that shit.

"Oh, shit, look at the time!" I yelled, causing Bruce to wake up.

"What's wrong, baby?"

"I missed my curfew, and my mama gon' be tripping."

"I thought ya home girl had you covered?"

"I'm sure she did, but I need to get home before she sends my brother looking for me," I said while getting up and getting my clothes on.

When I finished, I kissed his lips and headed for the door.

"Hold on, ma. Let me at least walk you to the car." Bruce hopped up and threw some clothes on, then slipped his feet in his Yeezy slides so he could walk me to the car.

As soon as we made it out front to my car, we stood on the side and talked for a second until a car pulled up.

"So, this is why you can't come pick your fucking kids up?!" a chick yelled before she even got out of the car.

"Come on, Eve. I know you didn't come over here with this bullshit. It's late as hell!" he yelled while opening the door for me.

As soon as she hopped out of the car, I knew exactly who she was. I didn't want her to see me, so I hurried and peeled off before Bruce even had the chance to say bye. Now I was shitting bricks because I now knew that his baby mama was Eve, which was my brother's ex, and I hoped her ugly ass didn't see me. I was breaking every traffic violation speeding home, hoping to God I didn't get pulled over. I made it home in exactly ten minutes, and my mama was standing out on the step. I parked my car behind hers and walked up on the porch.

"LaVonya Marie, what the fuck is wrong with you? I know one thing. You better not get the fuck pregnant. I ain't about to play with ya little hot ass. I just hope you used something. I keep telling you these fucking boys can wait. You need to finish school; you need to be with a tutor, and I know damn well Sy dumb ass wasn't helping you with shit," my mama snapped.

I knew I was caught, so I knew it was no use in lying.

"I'm sorry, Mama, and I swear I was careful. It won't ever happen again. I promise you that," I said while standing right in front of her.

"I know it won't happen again because if it does, you will be living with your daddy, and I mean that shit," she snapped while letting me walk past her.

The minute my back was completely facing her, she smacked me right in the back of my head.

"Play with me again, and I'mma punch you in your fucking face next time."

I didn't do shit but walk off and make my way to my room with tears in my eyes. I knew she was mad, but she didn't have to hit me. I rarely got in trouble, and I was mad because I was off my shit over some dick.

Once I made it to my room, I laid across my bed crying like a baby. I knew I had fucked up, but I knew deep down inside I wasn't going to leave Bruce alone because that was just how much I was feeling him.

"Are you ok?" January asked while standing in my doorway.

"No, I'm not, but I'll be ok. Come in and shut the door."

Once she was in the room, she pulled me in for a hug and held me while I cried. I think I was more so hurt because I wasn't used to my mama reacting this way. But I must say I had a feeling it was coming since she had been calling me and asking me questions for the past couple of weeks. My routine had changed, and she knew what the deal was.

"You have to be more careful. You know Mama Vickie is watching us hard as fuck because we are beautiful young ladies. I know this because she tells me this all the time. You may think she not paying attention, but she really is. Now stop crying and tell me how it was." January giggled, and I did the same.

"He was amazing, and I really enjoy his company. I just know Frost and my daddy are not going to approve of this because he's a street dude."

The way January sat there in silence had me wondering what was going on in her head. Often, she would drift off when we talked, and I was starting to wonder what the fuck was going on.

"Well, finish school and graduate with honors, and once you're done and grown, you can date whoever you want," January said, being honest.

"That's true, but tell me about you and your love life. Was there anyone before you came here to live with us?" I asked.

January looked at me while holding her head down. I knew something was wrong with her, but I just couldn't place my finger on it.

"No. I've never had a boyfriend before," she said just above a whisper.

"Are you serious?" I looked at her with a raised brow. I just had a hard time understanding that a girl as fine as her never had a boyfriend.

"Yes, I'm serious. I've never been able to. My mama felt like having a boyfriend was a waste of time when you could have many men, give them what they want, and your pockets stayed laced. According to her, *'Having a little pissy boyfriend won't do you no good. You need a real man with real money to take care of you. Growing up and living in my house, you have to go by my rules. My motto is, money make you cum, and don't you ever forget it.'*

"So, yeah, that was my childhood, and it started when I was fourteen, so I don't know what it is like to have a real man care for me. Hell, I don't know what it feels like to live with a loving family. So, Vonnie, cherish your mama, and make sure you abide by her rules. If you wanna see your friend, just make sure you do that on your available free time."

Hearing everything January just told me made me put a different light on my situation. Plus, it made me look at how strong January truly was. Through all of this, she still managed to go on with life and get through school with great grades. Most people in a situation like hers wouldn't have made it this far. She truly had me looking at her different.

The sound of her sniffling brought me out of my daze. I didn't even know she was crying. I pulled her close to me, and we hugged while crying in each other's arms. I couldn't believe her mama was such a monster like that. I would hear and see about shit like this on TV, but to actually know someone, was heart breaking.

"I'm so sorry this happen to you, January, but now you're in a better place, and it's only up from here. No one will ever hurt you again, and if they do, they'll be handled," I said to her, being honest.

No words were spoken. We just held each other. I never had a sister before, but this feeling was everything, and I was happy January was able to open up to me.

EIGHT

Dalton

I was sitting at the table in the hotel room waiting for Vickie to come. The sound of the hotel door opening brought me out of my thoughts. I sat there and looked at her until she made her way all the way in. I knew she was about to start with her smart-ass mouth.

"I keep telling you we can't be meeting up like this. You always want what you want, and I keep telling you that's not how it goes, Dalton," she snapped as soon as she walked in the door.

"Vickie, don't come in here with all that fussing. You already know what it is."

"Dalton, you don't have no say so in my life. I thought I was a married woman?" she sassed while holding her hand up, showing me that cheap ass ring her sucka ass husband bought.

"Vickie, you come in here complaining all the time, but you still be bringing your ass here. Nobody told you to marry that fuck nigga, anyway. I let you get your little divorce, then you went against the grain and gon' marry somebody."

Vickie and I started having problems when I decided to make a little extra money on the side, other than being a police officer. Then, when I got Frost involved, she hated me even more. But the love we have wouldn't let us leave each other alone. I know I'm being selfish by not letting her live happily ever after with her husband. But I was still pissed they got married, so fuck that nigga. Plus, I knew if I didn't initiate this, Vickie wouldn't even bother.

"You right, so guess what? This will be my last time coming, so don't ask me to come no more after today, and I mean that shit, Dalton. Since you are talking shit."

Not wanting to hear her smart-ass mouth anymore, I got up, lifted her up in my arms, and threw her onto the bed. The look she gave me showed me she was ready for whatever I had coming her way. I pulled her jacket off, then I unbuttoned her blouse while I placed soft kisses on her neck. Once her blouse was opened, I snatched her bra off, getting excited. I didn't know what it was about Vickie, but she'd always had me feeling some type of way ever since we were youngin's.

I eased my way from her neck to her breasts. I placed one in my mouth, sucking one at a time. I lifted up and started to take all of my clothes off. While I did that,

Vickie finished getting undressed while we both gave each other an intense look. Once we both were naked, I lifted her up, and she wrapped her legs around my waist. I then walked her over to the wall that was next to the bed and planted her back against it.

Once I was poking at her entrance, I felt her tense up, like she always did when I was about to enter her. She had to adjust to my size, but when she did, it was all love.

"I got you, baby," I assured her like always. I placed soft kisses on her neck while I entered her nice and slow.

"Mmm...Hmm...Dalton, just like that, baby." Vickie moaned out in pleasure while I hit her with nice, slow strokes.

Her tightness had me in heaven, and my eyes rolled back in my head while I moved in and out of her, steadily giving her them nice, deep, long and slow strokes that she loved. I sped up a little, but then I slowed down just a little more. I continued my method until I felt her pussy tighten on my dick, along with her digging her nails in my back.

"You are enjoying this dick, ain't you, baby?" I asked while drilling in and out of her wet ass pussy. I then decided to slide my finger in her ass hole while I hit her G-spot. I could tell by the way her body started to react that she was about to wet my dick up.

"Ohhhhh…Dalton, I'm about to cum…I'm about to cum!"

"Alright, well, come on, baby, and I'll follow right behind," I said in a husky tone while giving her faster strokes.

After we both came long and hard, I walked her back over to the bed, then laid down next to her. I kissed her forehead, and she smiled at me.

"Oh, so you not mad at me anymore?" I chuckled.

"I'm still mad at you because you don't care about anyone but yourself, Dalton. I know I'm just as wrong in this situation as you are. But you don't have anything to lose. I have everything to lose."

"What do you have to lose, Vickie? Because if you are talking about that weak ass husband of yours, you know I don't give a damn about him."

"See, there you go always on bullshit. I'd have to deal with another broken home, and I don't want that, Dalton. Not to mention, our son would have a damn fit. You already know how he feels about us dealing with each other. He was around all of the times you hurt me, and he's seen all the crying, the arguments, and the fights. My baby seen it all, which is why his relationship with you is not the best."

"Vickie, Frost is a grown ass man. What we got going on is none of his concern."

"An attitude like that is the reason you two will never really get along."

Vickie was really getting on my fucking nerves tonight. I just gave her ass some good dick, and she still fussing. Something must have been going on with her.

"What's up? Do you wanna talk about it?" I asked.

"Dalton, what the fuck are you talking about?"

"Come on, Vickie. You know I know you like the back of my fucking hand. I know when something is bothering you. So, tell me what the fuck is on your mind."

"Your daughter is driving me crazy, and you need to talk to her. I sit back and think about how we give her the world, and she just be cutting up. January is doing so well, and she's a kid that's been going through so much. But yet and still, she's doing so well. I hope when she tells Vonnie her story it helps her. Because the other night, I was about to knock Vonnie's head the fuck off. I told her one more mess up, and she's moving with you, so get her room ready."

"What you mean? What happened?"

"She thinks she's grown—that's what happen. So, talk to her, and she'll tell you what she been doing, herself."

"Why you can't just tell me?" I asked, being curious.

"Because I'mma let her tell you. You know y'all have the father-daughter bond just like Frost and I have a bond. Vonnie has always been closer to you."

"Alright, I'll talk to her tomorrow. Now how much longer do I have you?" I asked while pulling her close to me.

"The rest of the night. He's on the road for the weekend."

I pulled my ex-wife close to me right before I kissed her forehead. "I love you, Vickie. No matter what, I'll always love you," I assured her while kissing her once more. I knew I wasn't shit, and I knew I had a whole bunch of bad shit going on in life, but the one thing I knew for sure was that I loved my Vickie and my kids. Even if Frost

didn't think so, I really do.

NINE

I was finally moving into my own shit today. I had found a big ass house in the city, and I was happy as fuck. I was mad that Dalton didn't get my place for me like he was supposed to, but that was cool. Haas and I had been making bank since I got home.

"This place is dope as fuck. I can't believe they have houses like this in the hood."

"Right. I saw the shit and was amazed. They were acting funny as hell about giving it to me until I pulled out all the fucking money upfront. I swear, money talks and bullshit walks."

"You damn right, so how about we have a party this weekend to celebrate our new beginnings?"

I usually don't be doing all the partying shit, but I felt like I needed to shine a little and to have a little fun. Instead of always work and no play.

"I guess we can do that since I'mma be working on getting it furnished all week. By Friday, shit should be straight. You can go head and get the DJ, food, and guest list on and popping. I'll handle getting the place decorated. I already got furniture coming tomorrow for every room."

"I already got shit in play," Haas said with a dumb ass smirk on his face.

"Nigga, how did you know I was going to say yes?" I chuckled.

"I didn't, but I was going to get it popping, anyway. We been working like a muthafucka. We need some fun out the deal," Haas said, being truthful.

My phone ringing brought us out of our conversation. When I saw it was Eve's ass, I sent her straight to voicemail. She was really starting to be on some stalking shit, and I was growing tired of that bullshit.

"This bitch is starting to be in the way."

"Who are you talking about?" Haas asked.

"Eve, man. She be tripping all the fucking time. She not even my girl, so I don't know what the hell her problem is. I wonder where the fuck that baby daddy of hers is so she can leave me the fuck alone."

"Yo', you just made me remember some shit I was supposed to tell you the other night. Guess who the fuck that hoe baby daddy is?" Haas asked with a raised brow.

I laughed at the way his dumb ass was looking at me before I asked, "Who, nigga?! Looking all stupid," I said while shaking my head.

"Bruce ugly ass. Chuck saw them at the AMPM the other night. I meant to hit you, but I was with Simone's sexy ass."

"Wow, small fucking world. I already don't like that dude, and he don't like me, either. I'm really leaving her ass alone. I don't need no beef with that sucka ass nigga. I already feel like he gon' test me, anyway."

"I wish he would start some beef over that loose pussy ass hoe. Them kids look like Lucci from over the bridge, anyway. She started messing with his ass a couple of months after you got cased. So, I'm still trying to understand where Bruce ass came into play. I used to call her sis, and I thought she was loyal to you. Her pussy must have been thumping the minute you got locked up."

I saw Eve in another light too. I never thought I would come home and she would have kids. I knew it was something when she stopped writing me. I didn't want no visits, but I did write back when she did write. I guess she got pissed off when I didn't want her to come visit me. I liked Eve a lot, but I didn't love her. Love was something I tried the stray away from because I didn't need no distractions with the life I lived. But when I was done getting this cake and securing my future, I would definitely be looking for someone to share my world with.

"I thought she was loyal too. I was shocked to see she had two kids on a nigga, but it is what it is. I'm a young nigga, and I ain't ready to settle down just yet. All I know is, I was glad when she told me them kids weren't mine."

"Shit me too because you would have had to deal with that hoe for another eighteen years." Haas chuckled.

"Yo', you too damn much at times. I'm about to be out and go check the traps. Do you need me for anything else?"

"Nah. I'm about to sit here and make a couple of calls, then I'm gon' check up on my mama. I haven't seen her in a couple of days. So, just hit me up if you need me for something."

"Ok, be safe, bro," I said while Haas dapped me up.

The minute I was about to call and check on my furniture order, my phone started to ring.

"Yo', who this?"

"Hello, this is January! Sorry to bother you, but can you pick me up from work again? Vonnie's not picking up, and Mama Vickie has a meeting with Cade's case worker."

"Hey, Miss J! Ok. What time you get off?"

"I get off in an hour."

"Alright, I got you."

I don't know why I had a huge smile on my face by the time I hung the phone up. Then my mind wondered to where the hell my sister was. It seemed like lately, she was quiet and missing in action. That only meant it was a dude involved, and I made a mental note to myself to have a little talk with her when I saw her. I shot her a text letting her know that we needed to talk when I got there. After I sent the text, I just made a couple of phone calls, then locked my new home up and headed to the mall to get January from work.

January's job was only fifteen minutes away from my home, so it didn't take me long to get there. I sat in the parking lot waiting on her to come out. It was exactly time for her to get off, so I knew she would be coming out soon. While I sat and waited for January, I saw Eve and Bruce coming out the mall, walking hand and hand. I couldn't do shit but laugh since the bitch had just been blowing me up like crazy.

The sound of Miss J tapping on my window brought me out of my thoughts. When I looked up and saw a smile on her face, it caused me to do the same. She didn't smile often, and I didn't understand why because her smile was so breathtaking. I hopped out of the car and ran around to open the door for her.

"Hey, Dahmere!" she said, calling me by my first name.

Usually, everyone called me Frost, which was my last name, but the way Dahmere rolled off her tongue did something to me.

"What's good wit' you, Miss J?"

"Nothing much. Thanks for coming to get me again. I really appreciate that. I need to hurry up and get the bus schedule, so I won't keep bothering y'all to pick me up."

"Nonsense, girl. Everyone in the family has a car. It's no reason why someone can't come get you."

"I know, but I don't like to bother people. Which is why I'm saving to buy a car."

I felt bad because she didn't have any family to help her with these things. Her parents were supposed to be around to get her a car. Especially since she was such a good student. I loved how she was openly talking to me today, and it made me see a different side of her.

"You're not bothering anyone, so don't think that. Are you hungry?" I asked.

"I can eat. Why, are you hungry?"

"Yes, that's why I asked. You ever been to Texas Roadhouse?"

"No. I haven't really been many places. My mama would only let me go to school and come straight home."

"Alright, well, that's where we headed to," I said while starting the car up, then peeling off.

January and I had been texting on and off since we had dinner. I knew I shouldn't have been texting and talking to her, but it was something about her that had me wanting to know her story. I knew my mama would be feeling some type of way if she knew, but it wasn't even like that with Miss J and I. I just loved to see her smile, and I hated seeing her down a lot. So, if I could keep a smile on her face, then that's what I was going to do.

"The DJ is here, ready to set up," Haas said while walking into my room.

It was Friday, and the house was finally furnished. Haas had got everything ready for the party, and we were finally about to get this shit started.

"Ok, cool. Did my mama bring all the food yet?"

"She down there, too, setting up. She told me to come get you. January is down there with her."

Hearing January's name caused me to jump up. I didn't even know she was coming to help my mama. I was hoping she would come back. I knew Vonnie was coming, but January wasn't like that. Big crowds weren't her type of thing from what she told me.

Once I made it down to the kitchen, I pulled my mama in for a hug. Then, I did the same thing to Miss J.

"Hey, y'all! Mama, what you cook?" I asked.

"Four different type of wings, meatballs, sautéed shrimp, and a pasta salad. You said you wanted finger-foods, so that's what I did. I figured you would want a salad with it, so I did pasta."

"It all sounds good. Thanks, Mama. You know I appreciate you for doing this for me."

"You know I got you, baby. Just do me a favor and stay safe. Is Vonnie coming tonight?"

"She said she was. I was hoping that January would come back with her."

"Are you coming out to have some fun, baby?" my mama turned to her and asked.

She looked at us both and hunched her shoulders, letting her know she didn't know. I knew that's what she would say, but I knew for sure I was going to hit Vonnie up to get her to come out and have a good time. A girl her age didn't need to stay cooped up and sad all the time.

"Well, if you feel up to it later, you're welcome," I said, being honest.

After her and my mama set the food up, they left, and I was about to go get myself together before the guests started to arrive. I didn't know who all Haas invited since I left everything up to him. I just wanted tonight to be good music, food, and drinks with no damn drama.

"Yo' mama be hooking shit up. Why she don't start catering?" Haas said while picking up a wing off the platter.

"I don't know. That's something I'mma talk to her about. That could be one of the things on my to-do list—something added to my future plans. I want my sister and my mama to be comfortable just like me. So, yeah, I'm on it. I'm about to go get myself together. Did Poppy put some of his men at the door?" I asked, referring to my Godfather.

He had his own security detail business. So, I had contacted him to put some of his men out in front of my house.

"Yeah. Everybody and everything is in place."

"Ok, cool. Let me go get dressed. I'll be back in a little bit. Hold shit down 'til I get back."

Haas and I dapped each other up, and I headed upstairs to get dressed. Even though I didn't usually do all of this, I felt kind of proud of how shit was going on right now for me, and it was time I enjoyed the fruits of my labor.

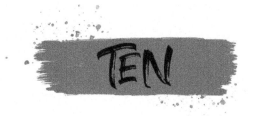

TEN

January

I was a little nervous about going to Dahmere's party, but Vonnie had talked me into going. So, I figured what the hell, why not go? The sound of a knock on my bedroom door brought me out of my thoughts. I jumped up and answered the door.

"Hey, girl! You look so cute. I told you them jeans would fit you goodt! Are you about ready to go?"

"You look cute too, and yes. Just let me put my hair up in a messy bun, then I'll be ready to roll out."

I had on a pair of ripped jeans and a black crop top. Then, on my feet, I had on the Chuck Taylor All Star GR82's. I didn't do makeup, so I had a little lip gloss on my lips. I grabbed my basketball satchel bag, and Vonnie and I headed out the door.

"Y'all be safe, and call me if you need me," Mama Vickie told us while we headed out of the door.

Luther still wasn't home, and shit had been seeming a little suspect between the two of them lately. They never argued in front of us, though. So, we really didn't know what was going on. Most of the time, he was on the road for work, so maybe he was just working. I didn't know, though, so for the most part, I just minded my business.

"Ok, Mama. We gon' be good, and Poppy is there. You know he don't play about Frost and I," Vonnie said, referring to her Godfather, Mr. Louis.

Vonnie and I hopped in her car. After I put my seatbelt on, I hooked my phone up to the car and turned some music on. I was in the mood to have a good time, and that was exactly what I was going to do. I didn't really hang out, but for once in my life, I wanted to have a good time. I felt pretty, and most of all, I felt comfortable around my new family.

Ten minutes had gone by, and we were now pulling up in front of Dahmere's new crib. It was so many cars outside, and the security was on point. Once Vonnie parked the car, we hurried up and hopped out. Mr. Louis was in front of the house. Vonnie and I both gave him a big hug before we went inside. Before I walked in, there was a dude standing behind Louis staring at me. It had me feeling a little uneasy, but I just let it go and walked inside the house.

The minute we walked in the house, Vonnie stopped in the middle of the floor and started dancing. I didn't even know she could move like that. She was getting it, and the crowd was going wild.

"That's my bish!" I heard from behind me, and it caused my face to turn up.

I turned to face exactly who I knew it was. I didn't care for Sy, but of course, I kept it cordial because she was Vonnie's best friend. They hugged each other and then both started dancing.

"Don't worry, you aren't the only one that don't care for her little hot ass," Dahmere said while walking up behind me. The way he grabbed my waist had me feeling some type of way.

"Wow, is it that obvious?" I giggled while turning to face him.

"Yup, I saw it all in your face the minute you heard her voice. Come on, so I can get you something to drink and some food."

"I don't drink."

"You drink soda, juice, and water, don't you? I hope you didn't think I was going to give ya little young ass no damn liquor. My mama would kill me." He chuckled.

"My bad. I thought that's how these parties be going down."

"Yeah, that's how they be going down, but my sisters and her friends ain't drinking no liquor on my watch. If they look lit that's because they got lit before they showed up."

Dahmere and I headed into the kitchen. When we made it in there, Haas was in there. Looking high as a kite.

"Hey, January! What's good with you, beautiful?" Haas spoke.

"Hey, Haas! I'm good. I came out to show y'all some love. This place is nice. Y'all did a great job on it."

"Nah, this Frost shit. I'm just a visitor. This going to be my home away from home, though. But let me go party. I'll see y'all around."

After Haas left out of the kitchen, Dahmere handed me a plate. I sat down in the chair at the kitchen table and started to eat while he watched me. Usually, I would feel uncomfortable, but never around him.

"Girl, I was looking all over for you," Vonnie said while walking into the kitchen with Sy following right behind her.

"Hey, sis! What's good with you?" Dahmere said while walking over to Vonnie and pulling her in for a hug.

"Hey, Frost!" Sy cooed.

"What's up, Sy?" he spoke, keeping it short.

I could tell she was feeling him by the way she was eye-fucking him. If they never went that route before, I could tell she damn sure wanted to.

"This is a nice place you got here. When you gon' invite me over for a private party?"

"Never. Now if y'all excuse me, I have to go entertain my guest. Miss J, if you need anything, baby girl, just come find me. Same go for you too, Vonnie," he said while making his way out of the kitchen.

"What I tell you about flirting with my brother?"

"You already know how we do. I'm sick of him acting like I'm too young for him. My birthday is in two weeks. I'll be eighteen. Shit, I'm old enough. He only in his twenties," Sy said while sucking her teeth.

"Girl, my brother ain't thinking about ya ass. You good, January?" Vonnie asked, causing Sy to suck her teeth.

"Yeah, I'm good. I'm just chillin'. When I'm finished eating, I'll be back out there with y'all," I assured them while taking another bite of my chicken.

The sound of someone walking into the kitchen could be heard after they left. I looked up, and it was the dude that was out front staring at me. I didn't say anything. I just turned and continued eating my food.

"I knew that was you when I saw you out front. At first, I wasn't sure because you all grown up now."

"Excuse me?" I said while turning to look at him.

"Little Cookie, girl, you've grown so much. I need to contact Tracy to see what that going price is for today. It's been a minute, and I haven't seen her, but shit, I'm glad I ran into you today. What you like, seventeen or eighteen now?"

Hearing Tracy's name and him calling me Cookie caused me to get sick to my stomach. I jumped up so fast and tried to exit the kitchen, but he grabbed me by my jean pocket and pulled me back.

"Get off of me!"

"Not 'til you talk to me Little Cookie. It's rude to just walk away when someone is talking to you." He grimaced while placing his nose in the side of my neck.

"Get the fuck off of me!" I yelled while tears started streaming from my eyes.

"Shhhh…stop crying, Cookie. I'm just trying to see what that little pussy could do now. You were a lot younger when I first tried it out. Now you grown and more developed."

"What the fuck is going on in here?!" Dahmere yelled while walking in the kitchen.

The minute dude heard his voice, he let me go, and I ran right into Dahmere's arms while crying hysterically.

"I wanna go home… I just wanna go home…" I cried in his arms before he pulled me off of him.

"It ain't nothing going on, youngin'. I just saw a familiar face, and I just wanted to speak."

"Well, what the fuck is she crying for? You know what? Just get the fuck out of my crib before I forget you work for Poppy and kill your ass!" Dahmere barked, causing people to start running to the kitchen.

I was embarrassed at this point, and I just wanted to go home.

"Is everything alright in here?" Vonnie asked, but when she saw me crying, she ran over to me.

"I wanna go home," I cried while she pulled me in her embrace.

"Ok, pooh, come on. We can go."

"I know you ain't about to leave this lit ass party?" Sy asked with an attitude.

"Sy, can you just be quiet for once in your life? Apparently, something is going on here, and I need to get her home." Vonnie sucked her teeth as she grabbed my hand, and we walked out of the kitchen.

I was so upset that I ruined her and Dahmere's night, and this was one of the reasons I didn't hang out much. I never knew when I was going to see someone from my past.

Once we got in the car, Vonnie turned to look at me. She didn't even know what happened. She just grabbed my hand and told me it was going to be ok.

"One of the guys that my mama sold me to was there, and he remembered me. He said he wanted to see what this pussy could do since I was grown now. I didn't remember him, but when he called me by my childhood name and said my mama's name, I knew right then and there he was one of the men that she let touch me. How come I didn't remember him? Will I always run into men that had their way with me as a child? How the hell will I ever go on with life with such a dark past?" I cried while lying back in the seat.

"Your past will be one you'll never forget, but trust me, there will be someone that'll love you no matter what your past was. You didn't just get up and do those things, January. Your mama made you. You were taught that it was the right thing to do. Now you know better, so stop blaming yourself."

After Vonnie said her piece, no more words were spoken. She peeled off, and we made our way back home. I knew Ms. Vickie was going to wanna know why we were back so early, and I didn't mind telling her. It was the motherly love for me. Every time we talked, I felt like I was in a better mood. Sometimes, I believed God brought me here for a reason.

ELEVEN

LaTonya (Female)

I had been doing somewhat better in school, thanks to January helping me. Since I had been in the house and ignoring Bruce for a little bit, I had been able to study. I knew he was getting a little upset with me, but I knew I needed to get back on my mama's good side. So, I had to chill for a little bit. I made sure I texted him and called him often, but he just hadn't physically seen me since that night I missed curfew. I had been missing him like crazy, so today I decided to go straight to his house after school. That way, I could chill with him for a couple of hours without missing curfew.

"So, you miss me?" I asked while I laid in Bruce's arms.

"I do, but check this. I can't be going this long without seeing you. What's the problem? You old enough to have a boyfriend, so why can't I meet your mama? Maybe that way, she will be comfortable with you coming to see me."

Bruce was straight tripping. I wanted him to meet my family, but he would have to wait 'til I turned eighteen and was finished with school.

"About that...my family feels like boys should be the last thing on my agenda. So, I was trying to hold out on you meeting them until I get out of school, or until I turn eighteen. Either way, I want us to hold out."

"I'mma hold out a little longer because I'm feeling you. But I don't know about waiting until school gets out. I want us to be exclusive, baby girl," Bruce said while kissing my forehead right before loud noises could be heard outside of his house.

The sound of glass shattering caused us both to jump up. I was praying to God that was his car and not mine. Because I would hate to have to explain to my mama and daddy what happened to my damn car.

When we made it downstairs and to the front door, Eve was standing there with a bat in her hand. I didn't want her to see me, so I stayed back behind the door.

"Eve, what the fuck you out here doing, ma?"

"You not gon' keep playing with me, Bruce! I told you the other day when you were at my crib you not gon' keep trying to make me be faithful to you, and you out here fucking everybody on sight! That's not how I get down! Then you are fucking with a whole high school girl! Yeah,

I heard about it! You forgot my little cousins are still in high school?!"

Hearing her say that meant she knew who the fuck I was, and soon, Frost would know about Bruce and I.

"Man, Eve, I don't know why you feel like since we got kids together, we have to be together. Where the fuck is that a written rule? Shit, you can fuck whoever the fuck you wanna fuck. Just don't be having a lot of niggas around my kids. That's all I ask for. I'm just worried about my kids' well-being. You know the type of nigga I am, and I don't need nothing happening to my fucking kids because you worried about getting dicked down."

"Oh, so you think I be putting my kids in danger? If you worried about how the fuck I'm raising my kids, you can come get them, then! Give me a fucking break for a change! You just drop money off and spend a couple of hours with them! Nigga, that ain't the fuck it! Giving money don't make you a good fucking parent—just let me put that out there!

"And little girl, if you know like I know, don't get pregnant by his ass. All I got the whole relationship was broken condoms, broken promises, and a fucking broken heart! Yeah, the money was a plus because he does spend dough, but that shit doesn't keep you the fuck warm at night!" she yelled while making me think differently about Bruce.

I didn't even wanna hear any of this any longer. I made my way upstairs to grab my things so I could get the fuck out of here. The last thing I needed was the baby mama drama that came along with dealing with a nigga like Bruce. Yeah, I liked him, but he had to put Eve in her place before he could come at me again.

Once I had all of my belongings, I made my way downstairs and back to the front door, where Bruce was still arguing with Eve's stupid ass. I had nothing against her until she started cheating on my brother when he got cased. He gave her the world when he was out. The least she could have did was waited for him.

"Come on, Vonnie. I know you not leaving because of what she said?" Bruce said, walking behind me as I made my way to my vehicle.

"I could care less what she is saying. My issue is that she keeps showing up when I'm here. Bitches only act like that when you still giving them reasons, Bruce. I don't have time for any of this."

"Call me another bitch, and I'll beat ya little ass!"

"Yeah, ok hoe. Go on home with your kids and leave me alone. I'm getting in my car, and I'm gon' leave y'all to y'all lover's quarrel."

I was shocked that she still didn't mention who I was, and I was glad. I just got in my car and peeled the fuck off, not paying Bruce any mind yelling my name. He had to get his life in order before he saw me again.

Frost and I were at our Godfather's house visiting with him and his family. I loved Louis, Latisha, and my twin God-brothers, LJ and Lance. They were a loving family, and sometimes, I wished my family was as loving as theirs. When my parents got their divorce, the shit devastated me, and deep down inside, I've never gotten over it.

"What you in here thinking about, princess?" my Godmother asked.

"Can I talk to you about something without you telling anyone?" I asked.

"You can talk to me about anything, but just know if you wrong, I'm going to call your ass out on it."

"Where's Frost and my God-dad?"

"They are in the man cave talking, so spill it. What's going on?"

"I met this guy, but he's a street guy, and he wants to meet my parents. I told him he would have to wait until I was eighteen and finished with school. That way, no one could tell me who I can or can't deal with."

"First of all, you know your parents only want what's best for you."

I knew she was right, but at the same time, I wanted to do what I wanted to do. Especially if I'm grown.

"I know, but they also need to let me find my own way like they did theirs."

"I get you wanna find your own way, but you also need to listen to your parents too. Now you know I love you, and I want what's best for you. Make sure you are being safe and doing what you're supposed to do. That includes getting good grades, graduating, and obeying your parents. If this dude is stopping you from doing what you're supposed to do, leave his ass alone. Besides, you're still young, baby girl. You have plenty of time to find the man of your dreams. You're going to come across a lot of heartache before you get there. So, right now, stay young as long as you can, and be grown when it's time," Latisha said while kissing the top of my head.

I swear, my God-parents were the truth, and I loved how I could talk to them without any judgement. They just kept it real and let Frost and I really know what it was.

"Thank you, God-Mami. I really love our talks."

"No problem, baby girl! You already know you're my daughter. Vickie may have birthed you, but you're mine too." She smiled while giving me a wink.

"What you about to cook for us?"

"Yellow rice and beans, stewed chicken, beef and chicken Pastelitos, and plantains. You know I had to cook y'all something. When Louis told me y'all were coming, I figured I would cook y'all favorites."

"Oh my God! I'm so glad because I'm starving. I didn't have time to eat lunch today. I studied for my test while on my lunch break."

"Say what now?! My God-daughter was studying on her lunch instead of going to all the lunches?! I'm so happy to hear that!"

I looked at her in shock, wondering how the hell she knew I be going to all the lunches.

"Don't look so surprised. You know your mama calls and tell me everything. Just like I know about you missing curfew. Like I said a minute ago, if dude got you disrespecting your parents, you need to leave his ass alone. He ain't cheering you on, telling you to finish school first, so to me, he doesn't give a damn if you finish or not. I say all this to say, if he really cares about you, he will wait 'til you finish school, and he will encourage you to make curfew."

I guess she was right. Whenever I meet up with Bruce, it's always, "When I'mma meet his parents?" Or, "Why I stayed away so long?" But it's never, "How was school?" or, "Are your grades up?" Hearing her talk had me really in my feelings because I was really feeling his ass, but does he care about my future?

"You know what? I never even thought about things that way."

"I know you haven't. That's why I'm over here schooling ya little hot ass. Now go get cleaned up for dinner while I go call everyone else."

I went to go get cleaned up for dinner, still thinking about all we just talked about. I might not have liked certain things she said, but I knew she meant well, just like my Mama did. Both of their talks had me second-guessing a lot of my dumb choices lately.

TWELVE

Dahmere (Frost)

I was sitting in my Godfather's mancave. We had just finished dinner, now we were just chillin' and discussing business. First, we started talking about what had happened at my party with Miss J. Once he told me the story, I was devastated, and I wanted his ass dead. Any man that does shit that he did to a kid deserved to be dead. And if Louis didn't already tell me he'd handled it, I would have did it myself.

"You good, son?"

"I'm still fucked up by what you told me. That explains a lot of the reasons why she acts the way she acts. Lil' mama had a rough life. I mean, I knew some things about her, but I didn't know how serious her situation was. Damn, the shit is crazy, Poppy. It makes me want to rescue her from her own thoughts. It makes me wanna save her from her past," I said, being honest.

"I knew from the way you looked at her that you were feeling her. If you wanna proceed with her, make sure you are done with all your bullshit. She's a damaged young woman and deserves so much more than what she's already been through. So, if you ain't trying to give her that, leave her alone, son."

"It's not like that, Poppy. I feel the same about her like I do Vonnie. Just like a little sister; nothing more, nothing less."

"Yeah, okay. Who you trying to convince? Me, or ya damn self? I ain't no dummy, son. I already know what it is. Like I already said, if you not ready to deal with what comes with a young lady like her, leave her alone. Don't disturb her peace."

I didn't respond to the last statement he made. I just nodded my head, letting him know I understood what he was saying. "So, what you think about this business plan?" I asked, changing the subject.

"You know I'm not happy about you being in this street shit. Yeah, I know you grew up in it, but you know I've always wanted better for you. So, if this is a step closer to you giving it all up and thinking of a master plan, I'm all in. But you know Dalton is not going to be happy about this shit when he finds out."

"It is what it is. I hustled hard as hell to get where I am. And I'll be damned if I give him a cut when he ain't even do shit. I know that's what he gon' be coming at when he finds out. Which is why I want you to act like it's yours."

"I got you. As long as you fall through with your promise of not making this your future, then you have a deal. As a matter of fact? Let me come at ya pops and let him know I got some shit going with the pills. I'll even let him know that I gave you and Haas some to sell for me. Shit, all I'm doing is the same thing he's doing: trying to make some extra cash."

"Poppy, I'm done with all of this as soon as I get everything situated the way I want it."

"Ok, well, let me hear some of your business plans," he said, shocking me.

I broke down all the new business ventures I had in mind, and he told me which ones were great ideas, and which ones he didn't think were so great ideas. I loved my Godfather, and I was glad I had another male figure in my life besides Dalton's ass. We sat and talked for another hour or two before I headed out.

I dapped Poppy up and then went to give Mami a hug. That was the nicknames we had for Louis and Latisha ever since we were youngin's.

"I'm about to head out, Mami."

"Your sister just left. I don't know why y'all didn't come in one car. Get on over here and give me a hug." She pulled me in for a hug and held me tight.

I loved her and Poppy so much. That was one thing my mama and Dalton did right. They gave us the best God-parents ever.

"I love you, Mami!" I said, being honest.

"I love you more, baby, and make sure you be extra safe out there."

"I got you! I'm always safe." I smiled while going out of the door.

The minute I hopped in the car, my phone alerted me that I had a text message. When I looked at the phone, I saw it was Haas telling me to check the trap on 32nd. He said he got a video of these niggas playing when they supposed to be working. He even sent me the video that was sent to him. These niggas were going to stop playing with me. Since I've been home, I've been trying to keep my attitude straight because I didn't need any more charges. I was serious about changing my life around, and as soon as a nigga felt you were getting soft, they tried to play with you. I didn't have my burner on me, so I made sure to tell Haas to meet me at the trap. I knew he had his shit on him; he never left home without it.

I peeled off with my blood boiling, and these niggas were about to see just how mad I was.

Haas and I both pulled up on the corner of 32nd and Westfield at the same damn time. These niggas didn't even see us pull up—they were so into their card game. They had a table on the corner with chairs. They even had a couple of bitches cheering them on, making the whole corner hot as fuck. Yeah, they weren't in front of the house, but they were still on the corner of the block where my trap house was. Drawing all types of attention like some dumb ass niggas would do.

"Do you see this shit?" Haas asked while handing me one of his burners.

We walked up behind these niggas with our guns out. They were so into their card game they didn't even hear us walking up.

"Ladies, do me a favor and head out."

"Hey, Frost!" A familiar voice caught me off guard.

I turned and saw Yakeeta standing on the side of us. "Hey, Keet. What's good with you, ma?" I asked while signaling her over to me, then pulling her in for a hug. I knew I needed to be handling business, but she was a face I hadn't seen in a minute.

"I'm good, Frost! Especially since I just saw you. How about we get at each other when you done handling your business?"

"I'm all for that. Give me about an hour, and I'll hit you up. Put your number in my phone," I said while handing her my phone.

After she put her number in, her and her girls walked off, and I put my attention back on the fellas.

"Alright. Now, I need somebody to tell me what the fuck is going on out here!" Haas yelled while everyone was standing there looking at me like they were crazy.

I grabbed this dude, Ike, by his hoodie and pulled his ass right up out of the chair he was sitting in. "Is something wrong? Why the fuck all y'all looking at me like *I'm* crazy? Looking at me like *I'm* the one in the wrong," I asked while still holding Ike's hood in my hand while he dangled from it.

"They didn't expect for us to be here. But what they don't know is, we always got people on the lookout."

"Exactly!" I said, agreeing with Haas, "Now answer me this, Ike. Do I pay y'all to play cards?"

"No, Boss!" he said right before I hit his ass right in the mouth with the butt of the gun.

"I didn't hear you, my nigga! Speak the fuck up!" I yelled

"No...Boss!" he managed to get out as blood and his front teeth fell to the ground.

I then delivered another hit to the back of his head with the butt of the gun, causing him to fall to the ground. "I don't know what the fuck is on y'all minds, but I ain't the one to play with! Every one of you that thought it was cool to gamble while on my clock, get the fuck off my block, NOW!" I yelled.

They all started scattering and trying to pick the money up off the table.

"Aht-Aht, muthafucka. That ain't ya money. Put that shit back down," Haas said while pointing his gun at this nigga, Snoop, who was Ike's cousin.

I knew he was already salty because I'd used Ike as an example, but I didn't give a fuck. If they wanted to see me, they already knew what it was. I stayed ready.

"Come on, now, Frost. You gon' do me like that? I need to feed my kids," Snoop begged.

"One thing I hate is a begging ass nigga. Your ass should have thought about making money before you decided to be on my shit playing. Now get your cousin the fuck up and get the fuck off my shit."

Haas and I cleaned up the mess, then grabbed all the money that was on the table—plus, the money and the work that was in the trap and locked it up. Tomorrow, I would assign some new niggas on it. But tonight, I was going to chill and call Keet up. I needed some pussy too since I wasn't fucking with Eve's ass anymore. Plus, I heard her ass been popping my damn pills. I hated that shit, but she wasn't my girl or anybody I was fucking, so she wasn't any of my concern anymore.

"DAMN, GIRL!" I yelled out in pleasure while Keet was rocking my mic.

The way she was slurping, sucking, and showing my dick and balls love had me ready to wife her ass. But I couldn't do that shit with Keet. She was a money girl. Dollar signs made her cum. Yeah, I could fuck without paying her ass anything because she was feeling the kid, but just knowing the type of chick she was, I just kept it a sex thing. Nothing more, nothing less. Being the man of the streets had its perks, but sometimes, the shit wasn't everything. Fucking different chicks all the time was cool, but it got old. I was still young and had my share of women. I was starting to wonder where the good girls were at. The ones that wasn't just worried about what I could do for them.

I was moaning like a bitch—toes were curling and everything. If this was a contest, Keet would have won, hands down. I wasn't ready to cum just yet. I wanted Keet to cum all over this dick.

"Come on up here and ride my dick, ma!" I barked, causing her to jump right up.

Before she climbed on top of me, I handed her the condom that laid on my nightstand right next to the bed. The way she rolled her eyes I knew she wasn't feeling that, but I didn't know what the fuck she thought this was. I hadn't seen her little ass in a minute.

Once the condom was on, she straddled me. I then moved my finger across her clit, getting her wet and ready to slide down on my pole. The feeling of her sliding down on my shit nice and slow had my eyes rolling back in my head. Her head game had me distracted. I almost forgot how good her pussy was.

"Damn, girl...you nice and wet for me, huh?"

"Fuck, Frost! I miss this dick," Keet said while tightening her walls up on me.

I knew what her ass was trying to do, and I wasn't ready to cum just yet. I wanted to enjoy her insides for a little while longer. I grabbed a handful of her hair and pulled her face close to mine so she could hear me. "Stop playing with me, girl! I ain't ready to buss yet."

She looked into my eyes, giving me an intense stare while she continued to tighten her pussy muscles on my dick once more.

"Fuck, I'm about to cum, ma!" I yelled while shooting my seeds into the condom.

I could tell Keet was cummin' as well the way her body was jerking on top of me. Once she came long and hard, she laid on me, and I held her tight. Sex with her was always amazing. I just wished she was the type of chick that I could wife.

"Damn, that shit was good, as always, Frost," she cooed while kissing my cheek.

"You crazy, girl. So what's up? How you been? What got you back in town?" I asked, being curious.

"I was getting homesick and was missing my mama. So, I decided to come back and stay for a couple of months."

"How's shit going for you in Cali?"

"It's great. It's just hard as hell getting this business started."

When those words left her mouth, I knew what it was. Her ass was back in town to find a sponsor. I wasn't no dummy; Keet always had a plan. She had been modeling since we were younger. So, by now, I thought she would be more established, but I guess not.

"Keep pushing, baby girl! If this is a dream of yours, you'll get it on and popping," I said, being honest.

"I know, and that's a plan."

Before I had the chance to say anything else, the sound of someone knocking on my door brought us out of our talk. It was late as hell, so I had a feeling it wasn't anyone but Dalton's ass, and word must have gotten to him about what happened earlier. I hated when he thought he ran me. When he told me to gather my teams up, then he gave me permission to do what the fuck I wanted to do with my team.

"Stay up here, ma. I'll be right back. I'll bring you up something to drink when I come back up."

"Ok, no problem," Keet said while getting comfortable on the right side of my bed.

Before I got down the steps all the way, the knocks had grew louder. When I opened the door, Dalton was standing there with a mean look on his face—like I gave a fuck.

"Why are you banging on my door like that? What's this serious that it couldn't wait 'til the morning?"

"I can come over here whenever I feel like it. Now tell me why you haven't been to your parole officer? I told you before you only had to check in once a week, and why haven't you did it yet?"

I wasn't going to lie. I forgot all about that shit, but whoever my parole officer was, they were supposed to reach out to me, and not Dalton's ass.

"My bad, I'll call tomorrow. But whoever it is ain't doing their job because they didn't reach out to me. I forgot, being ass though I never had to see one before. Only this time because you couldn't stay on your shit and get me out of all this shit. I had to do two years, and now I have to go to parole. You got me working for you, and you can't make sure I'm good. The shit is getting old. Think about this Dalton. You may have other workers dealing with you, but I'm the only loyal one because I'm your seed. Now let that marinate."

He knew I was right, which was why he didn't say anything. He just turned and walked out of the door. I knew I was hiding what I had going on from him, but at the end of the day, I was loyal to him in other ways. Because when I was down, they always tried to get me to turn on his ass, but I never would. I didn't know what they thought they had on him, but apparently, whatever it was, they couldn't get it to stick, which was why they tried me.

Shaking that shit from my brain, I walked into my kitchen and grabbed Keet and I a water, then made my way back up to my bedroom. When I made it up there, she was knocked out, and her naked body could be seen through the thin sheet, causing my dick to brick up again. As much as I wanted to dick her down once more, baby girl looked peaceful, and I wasn't going to bother her. I just sipped my

water, then laid my tired ass down.

THIRTEEN

I was chilling with my kids and Eve all day, but something was off about her dumb ass. We had a nice night and dinner. I even dicked her down really good, that way when I left her, she would leave me alone for a minute. But it was like, ever since her ass got up, she had been on one, and the shit was driving me crazy. I was so happy when she went in the room to lay my kids down for a nap. It gave me time to get my blunt rolled and enjoy the peace of not hearing her mouth. I needed a lighter to light my blunt, so I looked in her nightstand drawer, where they usually were, and noticed a bag with 32nd and a snowflake on it. The shit angered me because I knew that symbol wasn't nobody's but that geek ass nigga, Frost's, shit.

Anger really came over me when the thought came to mind that Dalton was holding out on me. Shit, I wanted in on everything. Not just some shit. I had a family to feed just like everyone else. I know his loyalty laid with his seed, but damn. I was hustling for his ass when his seed was cased, and he promised me things wasn't going to change when Frost was released. Shit had been cool up until this very moment.

"Why the fuck are you in my drawer?" Eve snapped, walking into the room.

I was so into my thoughts I didn't even hear her come in. I threw the pills on the floor and watched her fall to the floor and pick her shit up like she was a crackhead.

"You popping pills now?" I grimaced.

"Mind ya fucking business, Bruce. You don't give a fuck about what I do, anyway. Shit, you sell drugs, nigga, so don't come for me."

"Eve, I didn't ask you shit about what the fuck I do. You be in here popping pills with my fucking kids? Is you crazy?" I snapped while getting up and snatching her ass off the floor. I snatched the pills out of her hand and headed for the bathroom.

"Bruce, give me my shit!" she yelled while chasing me into the bathroom.

"No! You been popping pills in front of my fucking kids, and you lucky I don't beat the shit out of you right now! You high right now, ain't you?! That's why you woke up on some other shit. Last night, we were cool as hell doing our family thing, and you wake up on good bullshit. Who the fuck did you get these from?" I asked, knowing she wasn't going to tell me shit.

"Why? If you gon' go get me some more, then I'll tell you where I got them from. If not, boy, fuck you."

"If you don't tell me where the fuck you got this from, I swear, on my mama, I'mma fuck you up, Eve."

"Oh, you mad-mad…Didn't I say, boy, fuck you?" Eve giggled while heading out the bathroom. "You don't have to get me anymore. I'll just go fuck the boss to get me some more. We good friends, anyway. We go way back."

I jumped on top of her ass, laying slap after slap on her face. I didn't even realize I had gotten that mad. The sound of my kids crying brought me out of my angered mood. It was a good thing they weren't in the room watching us. I left Eve's ass on the floor and ran to their room where they were in the bed holding each other. I guess the loud screams must have woke them up from their nap.

"Everything is ok," I said while climbing into the bed and cuddling with my sons.

Eve had a fucking problem, and I was going to pack my kids' shit up and take them to my mama for a couple weeks. I was sick of her shit, and I knew the life I lived I couldn't take them with me. So, my mama's crib was the next best place. Although I knew she was going to chew me the hell out, I knew once I told her the shit Eve was on, she wouldn't have no problem with taking my boys.

A couple hours later, I had gathered all the boys' things and dropped them off to my mama's house. I thought Eve was going to put up a fight, but she didn't. She just laid there on the couch like I wasn't taking her kids from her. My baby mama was tripping, and I was so mad at her ass. Hearing her say she can fuck the boss to get more had me fucked up. I knew the shit belonged to Frost, and I wasn't feeling that dude.

When she had said what she said, I put two and two together and figured out that Frost must have been her dude that she was fucking with before she met me. I remember her telling me her dude had to do a bid, and she wasn't waiting. I brushed all of that to the back of my head since I was now pulling up at the warehouse where we met up when we wanted to see Dalton's ass. I needed to talk to him to find out why I wasn't on to what he had going with the pill shit.

"Took you long enough to get here," Dalton said as soon as I walked in.

"My fault. I had to take my kids to my mama," was all I said before I laid the pill rapper on the table.

"What the fuck is that?" Dalton asked.

"I was wondering the same fucking thing. I wanted to know why I wasn't up on this new venture," I asked in a sarcastic tone.

"What new venture? That ain't my shit," Dalton snapped.

"If it ain't ya shit, it definitely belongs to your son. So, how you don't know about this shit? I thought nothing happens in this city that pertains to the drug game without you being in on it?"

"How you know this is my son's shit? As a matter of fact, how you come in here blaming stuff on my son? Did he tell you himself that it was his?"

"He didn't have to. Look at the bag. It has 32nd and a fucking snowflake on it. Ain't ya son's name Frost? Don't he have a trap on 32nd street? Come on, now, Dalton, don't play dumb. Either you lying to me, or your son got one up on you."

He sat there and looked at me while stroking his beard. I knew he was pissed, but I didn't give a fuck. At this point, I knew he didn't know about it. But I still wanted to know why the hell didn't he know what the fuck his son was doing.

"Little nigga, I ain't never got to lie to you about shit. I will handle my son. You just make sure you are doing what the fuck you supposed to be doing out in these streets."

"I'm always handling my business."

"That's good to hear, but check this. I have a couple of men that I'mma put with you. It's about four or five of them. Frost fired them, and they still down to work. He fired them on some bullshit, so you don't have to be scared about hiring them. They're some good soldiers. Frost just wanna boss muthafuckers around."

"Ok, cool. Send them to my trap tomorrow, and I'll be sure to place them where more men are needed."

"Alright, cool, and thanks for putting me on to this because I really had no clue this was going on. I'll be sure to talk to Frost about it today."

Dalton and I dapped each other up, then I headed out the door. But the sound of his phone vibrating on the table got my attention and caused me to look at it. When I saw Vonnie's face flash across the screen, and the shit said

Princess, I was in shock. So little Miss Vonnie is Dalton's daughter and Frost's bitch ass sister?

So, this must be the reason why she didn't want me to meet them. They weren't going to let us deal with each other. This was going to be an open invitation for beef, and I didn't want that. But at the same time, I was feeling Vonnie. I was just giving her some space, but when I was ready, we were going to get back to the way we were. I knew she was pissed about Eve's ass. But she was just going to have to get over it. Especially if we were going to be together.

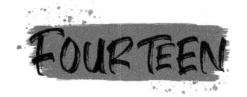

I was still a little embarrassed about the night I was at Frost and Haas' party. I was so in my feelings—I still hadn't talked to Frost about what happened. This was one of my biggest fears once I got out on my own. Dealing with situations like this. My mama had me with so many different men that I never know when I'm going to run into one.

The sound of arguing could be heard coming from downstairs, and it caused me to go running down to see what was going on.

"I don't know how long you thought you were going to go through this sneaking bullshit without me finding out! You thought you had one up on me, didn't you? So, when you gon' go back to his dirty ass?!" Luther yelled while getting in Mama Vickie's face.

"Luther, you don't even know what the fuck you are talking about. If you feel like I'm cheating on you, then why don't you fucking leave?"

"And make shit easier for both of y'all? Hell no! If he wants you, he can keep on getting you while I'm out of town! But when I'm here, I wish he would call your fucking phone! He thinks because he's a cop that somebody is scared of him! His ass bleeds red just like me!" Luther yelled while walking away.

Mama Vickie didn't say anything, which made me know that it must have been the truth. Luther walked by me, giving me a death stare like I was the one that cheated on his dumb ass.

"Is everything ok, Mama?" I asked while walking over to her.

"Yes, I'm good, baby. He just mad because he thinks I'm still dealing with Dalton."

"Well, are you?" I asked.

"Dalton and I are just friends. Nothing more, nothing less. He is the father of my kids, so we still have a co-parenting relationship."

From the way she answered me, it sounded like she was lying, but hell. She didn't have to prove shit to me. If she was still banging her ex, that was truly her business, and it had nothing to do with me.

"Are you hungry?" she asked.

"Yeah, I can eat. What you got for me?"

"Come on in the kitchen. I got some take out. I had gone past the Chinese store on my way home. I need food and wine, then my night will be complete."

Me and Mama Vickie sat at the table and talked about her day while we ate. I could tell something was bothering her, but I knew she wasn't going to talk about it to me. However, this argument made me put some things together. Like, her sneaking in some nights, and her staying out for days while Luther was on the road. I was shocked. Ever since I'd been here, they seemed like they were so in love. Now out of the blue, the arguing started. That meant someone was getting too comfortable, and now they got caught up.

I was about to ask her something, but Luther came into the kitchen with the boys following behind him. One thing about them two was, I knew they weren't going to argue around the boys.

I hated that I had to work after school today, being as though I was so tired after having one of my many nightmares. My shift was almost over, and all I wanted to do was head home, shower, then go to bed. After I clocked out, I headed to the food court to get me some Chick-fil-A.

"Hey, Holly! Let me get my usual," I said to the cashier.

"Okay, January, I got you. You off already?" she asked while she punched my order in the register.

"Yes, and I'm so glad because I'm tired as hell."

I was about to pull out my card to pay, but this dude that was behind me handed her some cash.

"Let me get that for you, beautiful," he said while smiling at me. He was fine as shit; I wish he would have shown his teeth when he smiled, but he didn't.

"Thank you!" I said while smiling back at him.

"You're very welcome."

Now that I was facing him, I could see that he had a missing tooth and a chipped one. I thought to myself why he didn't have his teeth fixed. He was dressed in all name-brand shit. Hair was cut, and not to mention, he had just paid for a stranger's lunch.

"Here goes your food, January," Holly said while handing me my bag of food.

Once I grabbed my bag, I hurried to try and walk away, but dude stood in front of me.

"Ayyye, yo'. You not gon' give a nigga ya number?"

Not really wanting to give him my number, I just told him to give me his. I pulled my phone out and acted like I was storing his number in, then once I was finished, I assured him I was going to call him later on tonight. I then smiled at him once more before I walked away.

"My name is Ike, January," he said while walking away.

If he thought I was going to call him, he was really crazy. Especially since I didn't even ask what his name was. I hurried and made my way out of the door, and there Vonnie was waiting for me. She had been looking down for the past week or so, and I wondered what was bothering her.

"Hey, Chica! How are you feeling today?"

"I'm okay. How was your day?" she asked a little too dry for me.

"You good? You've been looking a little down lately."

"Shit's just complicated between Bruce and I, but I'll be ok."

"Oh, ok. Well, I hope shit gets better between you and him. But let me tell you how this dude just bought my food for me. He was fine and everything, but the minute he opened his mouth, it was a turn off. Like, how you dressed in designer shit, but your teeth ain't fixed?" I giggled, causing Vonnie to do the same.

"Well, what was his name?" she asked.

"Ike or something like that."

"Oh, ok. Well, leave his yuck-mouth ass right where the hell he is."

After we finished laughing a little more, Vonnie started the car up, and we peeled off.

"Can I ask you something?"

"Sure! Go right ahead," Vonnie said.

"Your mama and Luther have been arguing like crazy. He thinks she's cheating on him with your daddy."

Vonnie looked at me with sad eyes. Right then and there, I knew something was wrong.

"Because she is. My mama been dipping with my daddy for a couple of years now. Luther dumb ass just now catching on. I heard them arguing last night. The crazy part is, I don't want my mama with either one of them. I love my daddy, but he just not good for my mama. And Luther? I don't know—just never really cared for him, but I always kept it cordial because my mama loved him."

Wow. I never thought that would have come out of her mouth, but it did. Since she already knew, it wasn't no reason for me to even entertain the conversation. So, I decided to ask her what was going on with schoolwork.

"How's schoolwork going?"

"It's going well, thanks to you. It's so much better when you study. I really appreciate you helping me, for real."

"I told you it's better when you know the work. You're really smart. You just didn't wanna ask for help. Never be too proud to ask for help if you need it. No one's perfect, and you have to know that we all needed help at one time."

"You're so right. I also think staying away from Sy has been a big help too. You know she's a bad influence. My mama would always say that, but I would never listen."

"Well, you already know how I feel about her, and I feel like she only sticks around because of how popular you are and because she wanna fuck Frost."

"Woooo, do I sense a little jealousy?" Vonnie looked at me and smiled.

"You know damn well we're like sister and brother," I said, trying to convince myself.

"Yeah, whatever!"

The ride home was a quiet one, and I was in my thoughts thinking if there would ever be a me and Frost.

FIFTEEN

Dalton

Frost was really starting to bother me, but there was nothing I could do about it. I needed him because like he once said, I really had no one that would be loyal. These young cats weren't raised up in this street shit like I was, so most of the time, they didn't know what the fuck they were doing. Since Frost wouldn't make it his business to come to see me, I made my way to his new home. I banged on the door a couple times before he opened. The minute he opened the door, he stared me down with a death stare.

"Man, I wish you stop popping up here like you pay my fucking bills or something. Then you be banging like you the fucking cops."

"Last I checked, I am the cops."

"Dalton, what brings you over here?"

"It's been brought to my attention that you got some new product that's being sold on my streets without my approval," I said while throwing the rapper that Bruce gave me on the table.

"Oh, this is Poppy's. He had given me and Haas some to sell. I talked him into adding my logo to the packaging, since it was being sold out of my traps. He told me when you came at me to send you to him."

"I'm definitely going to have a talk with him, but it's funny how you both start some new shit and don't tell me anything."

"Dalton, every man in the world don't have to run their ventures by you. You already have a lot going on being a dirty ass Jersey cop. Plus, this is Poppy we are talking about. You already know how he coming when it comes to you, and vice versa."

"It doesn't matter how he is coming. Either of you should have come to me. It was like y'all was being sneaky about this bullshit."

"Dalton, wasn't nobody being sneaky. I wish you stop acting like you're the only one in this world trying to make a dollar. You get on my nerves with that bullshit. You got me working for you and didn't even teach me the game the right way. All because you didn't want me learning and becoming better than you. Ain't that right, Dalton?"

"Frost, you will always be what I made you, son. And don't you ever forget it."

I could tell by the way Frost was laughing he really thought I was playing with his ass. Growing angry at him laughing at me, I walked up in front of him, placed my hand around his neck, and began to squeeze as tight as I could. Frost was going to learn not to fuck with me.

"Boy, I'mma tell you this one time, and one time only. I made you. You work for *me*, and don't you ever forget it. I'll take ya ass back to jail without a question," I said while letting his neck go, causing him to drop to the floor.

While he laid there gasping for air, I just stood there and watched him. I didn't know where the hell he had gotten all this courage and words of wisdom from, but he wasn't going to be trying to run me. I was so busy into my thoughts I didn't even hear Frost get the fuck up off the floor until I felt cold steal at my forehead.

"Because you my pops, I'mma let you live this time. But if you ever put your fucking hands on me again, I'mma shoot ya muthafuckin' ass, and that's on my mama."

The front door opening and Poppy walking in brought us out of our stare-down.

"What the fuck is going on in here? Frost, put that gun the fuck down!" Louis yelled while running over to us.

Frost put the gun down as soon as Louis told him too, which pissed me off, like always. I swear, it was like he was his son and not mine.

"I told you how he was going to react about your new product. Talk to him about it, then get him the fuck out of my house. The only time we need to do business is when we are handing off money and product. But other than that, you're dead to me, and I mean that shit, Dalton," Frost snapped while walking away.

"What the fuck was that all about?" Louis asked.

"You tell me what the fuck y'all got going on."

"I needed a couple extra bucks, so I started a little pill flow. I didn't think it would have you two at each other's throats. And before you ask why I didn't tell you, I was eventually going to, but it's small as shit, and you don't have to worry about it interfering with what you already got going on. I also asked Haas and Frost to sell it because you already know Latisha can't know what I got going on."

"I get all of that, but why wouldn't you contact me before you even got started on it?"

"Because I know how you roll, D. You think you the only one that's supposed to be making money out here in these streets, and I hate that you're that way. We grew up in these streets together handling business. Plus, you need to be leaving this shit alone soon. Like, when is it going to get too old for you before you lose everything?"

I should have known Louis was going to start with his little pep talk about me leaving the streets. I wasn't trying to hear shit he had to say. All I know is, I wasn't happy about them going into business without my consent.

"All I know is, if you plan on running this operation longer than a couple of months, I want a percentage, and I mean it."

"Oh, so that's how you about to do me? Like I never helped you before? You got some shit with you, and I ain't trying to entertain your bullshit. I'll finish up when I feel like it, and if you don't like it, do what the fuck you got to do, Dalton. But keep in mind, you already know how I get the fuck down. Not one muthafucker scare me, and ain't a bit of bitch in my blood. Friend or no friend, you better come correct when you come for me," Louis said while giving me a death glare.

No more words were spoken. I walked out of Frost's house while Louis stayed. He locked the door behind me, and I'm guessing he went in to talk to my son.

The minute I left Frost's house, I went home to shower. Then, I got a call from my Chief saying they had, all of a sudden, called a meeting, and I had no idea what the fuck it was all about. Lawd knows I wasn't in the mood today, and I was already on edge about the shit that had went down with Frost and Louis. A whole half-hour later, I was just now pulling up in the parking lot. I even saw the mayor's office had showed up as well. I also thought I saw the DA's car parked. I had no idea what the fuck was going on, but now I was intrigued. So, I hurried and parked my car, then headed inside.

"What's up, Frost? They all in the conference room waiting on you," the front desk receptionist, Trudy, said.

When she said they were waiting on me, I felt like this meeting was a case they wanted me to handle. As soon as I walked through the door, they were in mid-conversation, but what caught my eye were the photos they had of Bruce, Ike, and another one of the boys that worked for me.

"So, word is out that the dude with the black on is the ringleader of the trap operations. But we need the big man in charge. Whoever he is, he is very discreet. How we were able to find this much out was because of the Ike character. He likes to shine, so he spends crazy, throws wild parties, gets high, and is just always trying to be the center of attention. You already know what gets these cats caught. They always wanna be scene," my boss pointed out while he talked.

The minute he saw me, he gave me a head nod to greet me. I hurried and sat down so I could hear what else they knew. As long as I'd been doing this, they've found bullshit. But no concrete information, and especially no faces. This shit was crazy; Ike had to go, and Bruce had to lay low. This shit was about to fuck my shit up. At this time, I didn't need my money flow fucked up. This shit was the last thing I needed, but I had to do what the fuck I had to do before they placed all of this shit with me.

The good part about this shit was, they didn't have shit on Frost and his crew. Which meant they were handling they shit the way they needed to. I might've been mad at him, but at this point, I needed to lean on him a little harder until I found some new cats to deal with. I was going to have to fire Bruce and his crew, and I knew he wasn't going to like that shit, but it needed to be done. The crazy part was, I already knew this shit had to be because of Ike's ass. I should have just left his ass fired because I knew it had to be a reason why Frost got rid of him.

"Frost, I'm going to put you on this," my boss said, bringing me out of my thoughts.

"Ok, I'm on it, sir," I assured him.

"But, Boss, don't you think he needs to be working with someone instead of being by himself? This is not an easy case, and Frost is up there in age," Bryant Slone, one of the youngin's that worked for the department, said.

I couldn't stand his ass, and he always wanted to know why I rolled solo.

"I'll be fine, sir. If I needed someone with me, you know I would ask. So, to answer your question, youngin', I'm good. I've been my own partner for the past three years, and I don't need a new one now," I said, being honest.

When I lost my partner three years ago, I told my Chief I didn't need another one, and he abided by my wishes and let me work alone 'til this day.

"Slone, why don't you mind your business and handle your duties that I put you on? That's the biggest problem in the department. Everyone's always worried about the other. We all wake up every morning to catch the bad guys, and that's what we gon' do. No matter who's working with who. Now, next case we need to talk about is

Rodney Duvall. Word is, he gets out this week, and y'all already know what goes down every time this guy gets back on the streets.

"He's been down for a minute, so whoever these jokers work for stole his street cred. So, you know he is coming for whoever it is to get his shit back. Slone, I need you and Kelly to go check Duvall out today. Follow him around and see what he has up his sleeve. Maybe if we follow him, we can find the big fish in all of this. Frost, eventually, you and Slone will need to touch bases with each other, so please play nice," the Chief said, knowing exactly how I felt about having to deal with Slone.

Granted, he was a good cop. I just didn't like his little ass. I looked at Slone, with the dumb smirk he had on his face. Then, looked back at the chief.

"Okay, sir, I got you," I spoke.

But if Slone knew like I knew, he would stay the fuck away from me. Because I would hate for a cop to get killed in the line of duty.

SIXTEEN

I had to hurry and drop my kids off because Dalton had called for an emergency meeting. I had no idea what this shit was about, but I knew he meant business. Especially since he called it for all of us. We couldn't even go to the regular warehouse. We had to go to the one that was further out. So, I was anxious to find out what this was all about. Once I got to the warehouse, I saw that everyone was in attendance, even niggas I never even seen before.

Some big shit must be going on, and I needed to know what the fuck was about to go down.

A cranberry 2020 Challenger pulled up. The windows were tented, and the rims were everything. That bitch was clean as fuck, and I was dying to see who the fuck got out of it. When I saw it was Frost's ass, my blood started boiling. The fact that this nigga just got a new home and now a new car, I knew he was getting it, and I just didn't understand why the fuck Dalton couldn't get us hooked up with this pill connection.

Dalton had the nerve to tell me that it wasn't Frost's shit and that it was Louis' shit. But I wasn't buying that shit at all. This was Frost's shit, and if Dalton didn't figure out how to put me the fuck on soon, we were going to have a fucking problem. Once him and Haas got out of the car, they both walked over towards where I was. The death stare he gave me told me that me and this cat would never be cool. Which was fine with me. I didn't need to be cool with him to get this money.

I was going to become his brother-in-law soon, anyway. The thought of Vonnie came to mind, and the shit caused me to smile. She was acting funny lately, but I was going to get her little ass back. Vonnie was beautiful, and her pussy was A1. She was exactly what I needed to complete my life. After I pushed the thoughts of Vonnie to the back of my head, I made my way into the warehouse, where it looked like all the OG's of the streets were in attendance. I never even knew Dalton had it like this.

"Welcome everyone, and thanks for following instructions on how to get here. Today, I learned that we are on surveillance. The shit my boss told me had me angered, and today, by the time this meeting is over, there will be several men that will be fired. I suggest you take the money we'll give you and walk. Know that if you talk to the police, you will end up floating in the Cooper River.

"Since shit is getting hot, I have a certain plan that I want y'all to follow. I will be behind the scenes like I was from the beginning. Duvall is back out on the streets, but they're expecting him to take his shit back. When in all reality, this was always my shit. He worked for me. They just never knew who was behind the scenes. So, to know that they are close to finding out because of some dumb bullshit is crazy!" Dalton yelled while his yellow skin turned red.

I never saw him this mad, and I felt sorry for the dudes that were about to lose their life over this bullshit. I never understood why niggas didn't just stay under the radar and do what the fuck they were supposed to do.

"Hello, everyone. I'm Duvall, for the ones that don't know who I am. Dalton and I had a discussion before you guys got here, and this is how this is going to play out. All the traps on the Southside will be closed down. Out of each of those traps, a selective number of men will be shifted to all of the traps that Frost is in charge of. Bruce, Ike, Snoop, and Carl, get the fuck up here now."

I looked behind me as if he was calling another name, but nope. He was calling my black ass. We all headed to the front and stood there for a minute before Dalton walked up to us and passed us all an envelope.

"We will no longer need your services. I saw each and every one of your faces on the board at my meeting today. Why the fuck do the cops have pictures of your dumb asses?! You wanna know why? Because niggas like Ike wanna splurge and act like he big balling! The crazy part was, when Frost fired your dumb asses, I had compassion and figured I would move you all somewhere else!

"Yet, look at the mess you stupid muthafuckers made! I don't know where the fuck y'all going, but y'all can get the fuck out of here! And if I hear of any of you talking to the cops, I will make y'all watch me kill your mama, then kill y'all! Now get the fuck out of my face!"

Dalton yelled, talking to us like we were some bum ass

dudes, and I didn't like that shit.

I walked out of the door with my peeps following

me. I wanted to fuck Ike up, but I knew I was going to need

his ass. His cousin, Lucci, had connections, and we just

might have to move our shit over to Philly.

"Yo', I can't believe this shit. I should fuck ya

dumb ass up," Snoop said, charging for Ike until I held him

back.

"Man, chill the fuck out. I have a plan, and y'all all

need to be down, so we can get this money. Ike, can you

call Lucci to see if he has any spots for us out his way?"

"Man, my cousin ain't fucking with us because we

from out here," Snoop said, but I knew Ike had a better

relationship with Lucci.

"He may if we give him our money to put us on.

We also could tell him how they run the operation over

here. Maybe he could change up the game a little, and it'll put him on. We can also tell him about how the pills is popping over here. Then maybe he can find a pill connect over there," Ike said, causing the wheels to spin in my head.

"Good fucking thinking, Ike. How about we come to him with the pill idea all together and give him our money to get the pill supply? Then we bang that shit out real quick, showing him how fast the pills are doing the damn thing."

"I also fuck with a chick that go to Temple. Nobody pops pills like them high school and college kids," Ike said while a huge grin spread on his face.

"Alright. Since the traps were shut down, let's go to my crib and talk about this a little more before we give Lucci a call," I said, and they all were with it.

We all hopped in our whips and made our way to my crib. I always had a plan in my back pocket, even if I'd just came up with it. I had to keep my family fed, and I wasn't going to let Dalton and his bitch ass son take food out my kids' mouths. I had a plan, and these niggas wasn't going to be the only niggas in the world that were getting it.

The minute we got over Philly to meet with Lucci, he was all for it. The nigga even got us a pill supply right away. Now we were on Temple's campus at a party, and these college bitches were bad as fuck. The party was in full-affect, and everyone was dancing, drinking, popping pills, and getting fucked up off that White Girl. Ike was right: nobody got high like college kids.

"Yo', bro, this is Sanaa, the chick I told you about," Ike said while pulling this bad ass light skin chick with him.

Red bones were my kryptonite. And the way she was looking at me made me feel like she wasn't for Ike. She probably was only using him because of what he could do for her. Because the way she was licking them pink ass lips when he introduced us, Stevie wonder could tell I was going to be knee-deep in that pussy sooner or later.

"What's good, ma? I'm Bruce."

"It's nice to meet you, Bruce," she cooed while licking her lips.

I didn't do shit but shake my head. I couldn't believe that Ike's dumb ass didn't see the shit for himself. I was about to hold a conversation until Snoop came over to me and pulled me to the side.

"Yo', the pills I had are all gone. These bitches don't do shit but pop pills and suck dick. I dun' had my dick sucked by two of these hoes already." Snoop chuckled while shaking his head.

"Yeah, them pills must do something to their sex drive. Because these bitches be on one." I chuckled.

"That's what the fuck I'm saying. So, when do we reup?"

"I don't know. I meet up with Lucci tomorrow. He wanna know how we did, but check this. Do you know anything about that bitch, Sanaa?"

"If you trying to fuck her, double up because she's a loosey-goosey. I keep telling Ike to leave her alone. She fucks anything that got a couple of dollars. You don't even have to be bringing in the big dough, and she'll let you bend her ass over the hood of your car in front of everyone. I think she sucked the skin off Ike's dick and got him all in love. If I can fuck, then I know she a hoe. I'm his fucking family, but he not trying to hear me. He just thinks I want her ass, but truth be told, if I wanted her, I could have her. We prob could run a train on her nasty ass."

I laughed at Snoop, but I kind of already got hoe vibes from her, so I don't understand why Ike didn't peep it. "You wild for saying that dumb shit."

"I'm just being truthful. I'm going to go ahead and mingle. Hit my line when you ready to go."

"Alright. I'm trying to wait 'til everyone sells out, then I'll be ready. Show me the bitches that suck dick. I could use a good dick-sucking right now."

"Okay, follow me. These college bitches is nasty as hell. If they daddies knew what the fuck they were doing on this campus, I'm sure it would be hell to pay," Snoop said while shaking his head.

The shit was really mind-blowing how they got down in college. The shit made me regret not going. We mingled and partied for a little longer until we all had finished selling the product.

SEVENTEEN

The shit that went down at the warehouse yesterday was fucking crazy. To know that Bruce and the geek squad had been on surveillance was even fucking crazier. I hated to say it, but that's what the fuck Dalton get for hiring Ike and his cousins back. Obviously, it was a reason why I fired them.

"You hungry, baby?" Keet asked while walking into my room with a plate in her hand.

I didn't know why I had been keeping her around lately, but I knew I was wrong for this shit. I guess I wanted something more than to be in my bed alone when I got done hitting the streets all damn day.

"Yeah, I can eat. What you got for me?"

"I cooked some pepper steak and rice. I wanted to make sure you ate something before you go out today."

I didn't feel like going outside early today, so I had decided I was doing the night shift tonight. I wanted to check on these niggas that worked overnight in my traps.

"Thank you, beautiful! I really appreciate you. So, when you leaving to head back to Cali?" I asked, being curious.

I knew from the way her body shifted that we were about to have a conversation that I wasn't going to be feeling.

"I was thinking maybe I could stay here with you."

I knew this shit was going to happen. I knew she was going to get too damn comfortable.

"Baby girl, I'mma be honest with you. Don't stop what you got going on for a nigga like me. Yeah, we have good and fun times together, but I'm not trying to settle down right now."

"So, I'm only good enough to stay here so I can cook and fuck you?" she sassed.

"It's not even like that, Keet, so don't do that. You already know what type of dude I am, so don't be acting like you don't fucking know. Besides, I can cook for myself, and I could fuck any bitch," I said, not meaning for the word bitch to slip through my lips.

Me saying that struck a nerve like I knew it would, causing her to try to slap me across the face. I grabbed her hands and held them tight while I climbed on top of her.

"You acting the fuck up trying to hit me in my face. You need some act-right." I grimaced while I nuzzled my nose in the side of her neck.

I knew sex wasn't going to fix this conversation, but I also knew it would hold me over at this very moment. I looked Keet in her eyes, and we started to kiss each other passionately. We kissed for a minute before I pulled away. Once I did, I picked up one of her perky breasts and placed it into my mouth. I kissed, sucked, and slurped while I rubbed on the other one. Keet's attitude had went out the window, and now all she wanted was for me to do any and everything to make her cum.

I kissed on every inch of her body until I made it down to her pussy. I then started sucking on her clit gently, and all her juices started flowing. Keet stayed wet just the way I liked her. After slurping up all her juices, I decided to ease my finger into her wetness, while I moved my tongue across her clit in a fast motion. Her body started to jerk as I continued to move my fingers in and out of her as my tongue was still enjoying her sweetness.

"OH MY GOD! Frost, I'm about to cum, baby!"

"Go ahead, baby girl…cum for me," I said, watching Keet's body react.

After watching her cum long and hard, my dick stood at attention. I knew she was tired, but I needed her to take care of me, then she could take her fine ass to sleep.

"Come on, ma. I need you to handle this for me," I said while stroking my hard ass dick.

Keet straddled me, then slid down on my dick, nice and slow. She began to bounce up and down on my dick like this was the best dick she ever had.

"Shit, Frost, you feel so damn good inside of me…" Keet moaned out in pleasure while I matched her stroke for stroke from the bottom.

Keet and I went at it until we both bussed. Once we both came long and hard, she laid beside me, and I pulled her in my arms. No words were spoken. We just laid there enjoying the feeling of being in each other's company. I didn't know about her, but I was tired as hell and needed a nap.

When I woke up from my nap, Keet was gone, and she had left a note on my nightstand letting me know she would call me tomorrow. I knew she was still mad, but she would get over it one day. I was now out and about. All the traps seemed to be doing well. These niggas were on they best behavior. When I was finished, I made my way to my mama's house to see if she had cooked anything. A nigga was hungry as fuck. My mama's house was ten minutes away from the last trap I checked, so I was now pulling up. When I hopped out of the car, I noticed my mama's car wasn't here, and I wondered where she was at this time of night.

I parked my car behind Vonnie's, then hopped out. Once I locked my car up, I pulled my key out and let myself into my mama's house. Once I made it inside, it was quiet as hell, and I knew everyone was probably in bed. I walked in, and the light from the TV was the first thing I saw. I looked over to the couch, and Miss J was looking at me. I hadn't seen her since the shit popped off at my house. I smiled at her, and she did the same. I knew she was embarrassed, but after what I heard, it was no reason for her to be.

"Hey there, Miss J!" I said while locking the door before I made my way to sit down.

"Hey, Dahmere! What are you doing here?"

"I came to see what Mama cooked today. Where she at, anyway?"

"I don't know. She left here earlier after she cooked dinner."

"Oh, ok. What, her and Luther went out?"

"No. Luther is on the road this week."

After Miss J told me that, I knew what it was, and it caused my blood to boil. But I left it alone. I couldn't believe she was back dealing with Dalton's no-good ass. I don't understand how they didn't work when they were together, but she remarried, and now she good enough to mess with again. I hated when my mama put herself in situations like this.

"I hate when she put herself in predicaments like this. She knows his ass is no good for her, and here she goes falling for his shit again," I said while hitting my fist on the couch.

"I'm sorry for making you angry," January said just above a whisper.

"You good, lil' mama. It's not your fault, and you didn't tell me anything. I just put two and two together. Now what did Mama cook?"

"She made stuffed salmon, roasted potatoes, and broccoli. Come on in the kitchen with me, so I can make you a plate."

She got up and headed to the kitchen, and I followed right behind. She had on a pajama set, but you could still see her curves in it. She wasn't real thick. She was what you called slim-thick with some nice-sized, plump and perky breasts that I was sure was a C-cup. And don't let me get started on her little bubble butt. I laughed at my thoughts while entering the kitchen with her.

"Yo', I been wanting to talk to you about the night you were at my party. I know you don't wanna talk about it, and I know you may be embarrassed about it. I just wanted you to know you don't have to be. You had no control over the things that happened to you when you were younger."

"Thanks so much for saying that, Frost. I really appreciate that. I'm sure you heard about my past, and now you know why I'm so distant and don't like to be around groups of people."

"I truly get it now, and I'm sorry those things happened to you. You're definitely in a better place, and you should never be worried about anything ever happening to you like that again. If anybody ever hurts you again, or ever try, I'mma kill them."

Her silence had me worried, so I walked over to her to make sure she was ok. I could tell she was nervous with me being up on her. But I just wanted to make sure she was ok. She turned towards me, then pulled me in for a hug, and I hugged her back. I held her for what seemed like forever until she pulled back. Once she pulled back, we stared each other in the eyes right before we kissed. The shit felt like some magical shit, then the thought of her being my foster sister came to mind, and I pulled back.

"We can't be doing this, Miss J," I said just above a whisper.

"I know. I'm so sorry, Dahmere. Let me heat up your food so I can go back to watching my movie," she said in a soft tone while walking over to the microwave.

When she placed my plate in the microwave, she actually stood there and waited for it to stop, then she placed it in front of me. Then she poured me a cup of sweet tea and handed me my cup.

"Thank you, beautiful!" I said while winking at her.

Once she was finished, she made her way into the living room to finish watching TV, while I just sat and ate in my thoughts.

The sound of the front door opening brought me out of my thoughts. I knew it was my mama since Luther was on the road. I continued to eat until she walked into the kitchen.

"Hey there, son!" She smiled the minute she walked into the kitchen and seen me sitting there.

"Hey, Mama! Where are you coming from?" I asked, knowing she was going to lie to me.

"I was out with Carol."

I looked at her and started shaking my head. I knew she was going to lie. I just needed to ask to see what lie she was going to tell. "I can't believe you just lied to me like that. Mama, you don't even mess with Carol like that anymore. I know you were with Dalton, Mama. You don't have to lie. I don't like it, and I don't like him, but you grown. I just hope he don't hurt you because if he does, he has me to deal with."

"I'm good, baby! You don't have to worry about me," she cooed while coming over and kissing me on my forehead.

"I love you, Mama!"

"I love you too, baby! Make sure you do better with coming to visit me, and the boys been asking about you.

Maybe you should pick them up from school or something."

"Okay, Mama. I got you and them."

"Alright, baby. Thank you. Now I'm going to head to bed. Make sure you wash your dishes when you're done. And lock up when you leave."

"Okay, Mama, I got you."

I knew my mama would be okay, but at the same time, I didn't want her dealing with Dalton's ass. So I knew for sure I was going to pay him a visit.

EIGHTEEN

Since I had to pick January up from work, and I needed to do some shopping, I just went to the mall early. My daddy had just given me a stack, and I just needed a couple things. Since I had been trying to get my grades up, I hadn't seen Sy, being as though I was busy with school work. I knew she was pissed at me these days, but I didn't give a damn. If she was a true friend, she would understand why I was acting the way I was acting lately.

My phone vibrated in my pocketbook, getting my attention. I hurried and stopped so I could get it out to see who it was. I finally had got it, and when I looked at it, a smile crept upon my face. Bruce had been on my mind lately, but I had to keep convincing myself to leave him alone. Because dealing with him wouldn't be anything but drama. But I couldn't lie and say that I wasn't feeling his fine ass, though.

Bruce: *Hey, beautiful!*

Me: *Hey, you!*

Bruce: *You must miss me.*

Me: *Why you say that?*

Bruce: *Because you finally answered. Vonnie, I'm sorry, baby, and I would love to see you tonight. Do you think you can get away for a couple of hours?*

I stood for a second to get my mind right, so I could figure out exactly what I wanted to do. I missed him like crazy, but I just kept thinking about all the bullshit that came along with dealing with a nigga like him. But then I thought, *What the hell?* I'm not trying to marry his ass today. I'm just trying to have fun. I'm still young, and I have plenty of time to settle down with a real one.

Me: *I guess I can make that happen, but you need to make sure Eve don't come with no bullshit, Bruce, and I mean it.*

Bruce: *I already handled Eve, baby. So, you don't have to worry about her any longer.*

Me: **heart eye emoji* Okay, Bruce. I'll see you later.*

No other words needed to be said. The thought of seeing him later had butterflies fluttering through my stomach. After going into a couple of stores and purchasing everything I needed, I was headed to the food court to get me something to eat. The minute I made it to the Chinese spot, I saw a face I did not plan to see, and what shocked the fuck out of me was when she was walking with Sy—my "supposedly" best friend. Then I thought about it. I forgot Eve's little cousin attended our high school, but I never knew of Sy hanging out with the girl. I didn't say anything. I just kept walking right on past.

"Aht-Aht…Bish, I know you ain't about to walk right past me?!" Sy yelled, causing me to suck my teeth.

I didn't go over to her. I just stood to the side and made her ass walk over to me. When she did, her goons stayed back and waited for her to get finished.

"How can I help you, Sy? Wow, is this what we doing? You are hanging with the enemy now?"

"Vonnie, what are you talking about? I came to the mall with Tameeka. I didn't even know Eve was coming until we were getting out of our cars in the parking lot. Plus, you don't seem to be fucking with me these days, anyway, since you got ya new little foster sister."

I always knew she was jealous of January from the beginning. But I never knew that it would push her into the arms of other friends. I would have never thought that since Sy and I had been going strong since we were younger. My mama, daddy, and brother couldn't stand her ass, but they kept it cordial because of how I felt about Sy.

"So, this is what this is about? It's about me getting close to my foster sister? January is a good person. If you would just stop being a jealous ass and get to know her better, you would see that."

Sy stood there with her eyes rolling in the back of her head like she was annoyed by what I had just said. "See, the thing about that is, she's not my damn foster sister, so I don't have to be cool with her. No matter who I've meet, Vonnie, I've never kicked you to the side."

"Sy, I never kicked you to the side for her. I kicked you to the side to get my schoolwork done, and if you see me handling my business to secure my future, as a problem, then we don't need to be friends, Sy, and it's just that simple."

She looked at me like she was upset at what I'd just said, but at this point, if it ain't anything positive, then I have to leave it behind. I'm getting older and was about to graduate high school. I'm about to open up a new path in life, and that's the road to adulthood, and Sy just don't seem like she ready for that. She didn't say anything. She just sucked her teeth and walked back over to her new crew. And I walked off to go get my food before it was time for January to get off work.

The minute I walked into the line to get my food, Sy, Eve, and Tameeka were all behind me in line. I knew they were about to start some shit, so I hurried and pulled my phone out and shot January a text, letting her know what was about to go down.

"Well, look who it is. If it ain't the bitch that's fucking my baby father. Even after the bitch knew that's who he was, she still continued to fuck him. So, now I'm guessing I should call her The Homewrecker."

"Bitch, how would I be considered that when you weren't even wifey? Now I ain't about to argue with no hoe that was swallowing my brothers dick every chance she got about a nigga that ain't even hers. Now you know who I am and who my family is, Eve, and you truly don't want these problems."

"Hmm…maybe if I beat ya yellow ass, your brother would answer my fucking phone calls, and you would consider leaving my baby father the fuck alone."

"First of all, you ain't beating shit. Secondly, you really don't want them problems with my brother. Then last, but not least, you can fucking try me and get beat the fuck up, then I'll be sure to tell Bruce later on while we pillow talk, after he blow my back out, that his baby mama is nothing but drama, and she don't need her kids back. Now play with me if you want to, hoe," I spat with so much anger.

I could tell that she wasn't feeling what I said, but I didn't give a damn. I didn't know why Eve was acting like she didn't know who the fuck I was and how me and my brother got down. If my daddy didn't teach us nothing else, he made sure we knew how to protect ourselves.

"You fucking bitch!" Eve yelled while charging for me, then grabbing my hair.

The minute she grabbed my hair, I went the fuck off, throwing punch after punch right in her fucking face.

"Nope, bitch, you better not jump the fuck in it!" The sound of January's voice could be heard from behind.

We were in a full brawl right in the food court of Cherry Hill Mall. I'm sure somebody had us on WorldStar by now. My mama and daddy were going to be so fucking pissed, but I had to defend my damn self.

"Yo', what the fuck, Vonnie!" I heard right before I felt strong arms holding me back.

I turned around to see who was holding me, and it was Haas. I knew it wasn't the right time to think of this right at the moment, but the smell of his cologne had me thinking some other shit.

"Let me go, Haas!"

"Now you know I can't do that, baby girl. Come on, we have to get you the fuck out of here before the cops come. Dre, go get the video from the security office and tell them Detective Dalton sent you. Quay, get that raggedy bitch and her friends up off the floor and the fuck out of here. I already handled the security guards. I'mma let you go, Vonnie, but you better not try no funny shit. You too, January. Clint gon' let you go, and you better not try shit."

I didn't know how Haas was able to get the situation defused so fucking fast, but he did. We all walked out of the Mall, and I kicked myself for leaving my bags in the food court.

"Dammit, I left my bags."

"You good. We will go shopping next week and rebuy everything."

"Thanks so much, Haas, for handling this. Can you please don't tell Frost?" I asked.

"Lil' mama, he already knows. Why you think I'm here? January texted him when you texted her."

"Damn, girl, you weren't supposed to do that."

"Nah, she did right. If she wouldn't have, you two would be leaving the fucking mall in a cop car. I was able to get y'all out of there and grab the security footage, so they won't come back for your ass. So, tell me what the fuck are you fighting Eve for?"

"My fault, January. I guess Haas has a point. She always talking shit every time I see her ass. That's why we were fighting."

"Vonnie, I know you, and I've known you long enough to know that ain't true. I'm not gon' keep trying to get it out of you. I'll let Frost do that."

I was not looking forward to talking to Frost at all, but I knew my brother, and I'm sure he told Haas to bring us straight to him. I just sat back in the car and scrolled through my phone. Then I realized I was supposed to go see Bruce later on today. But after this situation, I decided not to. He still couldn't seem to keep his minion in her place. If they were done and nothing was going on, why the fuck wouldn't this girl just stay in her own fucking lane? I opened my messages from him and shot him a text.

Me: *Please lose my number. I'm sick of dealing with your bitch. If y'all are not together, why the fuck she won't find it in her to leave me the fuck alone?!*

Bruce: *Vonnie, what's going on?*

Me: *I already told you what it is. Lose my number, or I'll get my brother to make you lose it.*

Bruce: *Ain't nobody scared of your damn brother, Vonnie.*

After that last text, I deleted his old messages and then blocked his number. I was not about to deal with Bruce and his stupid baby mama.

I'd had a rough week. Between the shit going on in the streets and the case, I thought I was going to lose my damn mind. I had my Chief convinced that we were now at a dead end on this case. I knew he wasn't happy about it, but at the same time, I had to make it this way to save my own ass. The numbers were doing great since I had made all the right decisions.

"What's wrong with you?" Vickie asked.

"Too much going on in the streets right now."

"Do you think you'll ever stop?" she asked, shocking the hell out of me.

Vickie never got in my business about the street shit until I got Frost involved. She hated that I had him doing the same shit that I promised her I was going to stop doing. Her phone going off caught her attention, and when she looked at it, I knew something was wrong.

"To answer your question, I don't know if I'll ever stop. Now what's the long face for?"

"Luther knows about us. He just sent me a text letting me know that he was out front parked next to my car."

I jumped up and looked out of the window, since Vickie's car could be seen from the room, and Luther's nutty ass was sitting the fuck out of there like he was bat-shit crazy.

"How long has he known about us?"

"I'm not sure, but he just all of a sudden started acting like an ass."

"When you first noticed him acting crazy, you should have told me."

"I didn't want to because I didn't want you to be doing anything stupid. You know how you can be."

"I still deserved to know, Vickie. He could have ran up on me at any given moment."

I pulled out my phone, texted one of my boys from work, and called in a favor. I just wanted him to come arrest Luther for tickets or some dumb shit to get his crazy ass away from the hotel. Before I even laid my phone down, my guy, John, had texted back, letting me know he had me.

"I'm sorry, and you know Luther ain't even about that life. He ain't doing shit. I am concerned about Frost, though. You already know how he feels about you, and I just don't wanna lose my son over us linking up two-to-three times a week. The shit just doesn't make any since, Dalton."

"Frost is grown Vickie; he doesn't have to understand our relationship because it's none of his concern. You already know I will go through hoops to see you. So, how our grown ass kids feel is not going to bother me at all."

"I understand that they grown, but they are still our kids, Dalton."

"We don't have much time together before I go back to work, so can we please leave this subject alone? I don't want to start an argument."

"Okay. I have one more thing I wanna mention to you. Do you know your daughter was fighting at the mall?"

"Yeah. Now you know not much happens in this city without me knowing."

"So, why you didn't talk to her about it?"

"Her and I are having lunch tomorrow. So, I was going to talk to her then. Now enough about these damn kids. I wanna do some things before you have to go," I said while climbing on top of her and placing soft kisses all over her cheeks and neck.

Vickie giggled while my beard tickled her neck. I pushed everything she had told me to the back of my head. I didn't wanna worry. All I wanted was to feel my ex-wife's insides. While we kissed passionately, we both were coming out of our clothes. I was going to enjoy every bit of Vickie until it was time for me to go to work

Finding out that Vonnie was dealing with Bruce had me furious. Even though Frost didn't care for me, we would do anything to keep Vonnie on the right track. So, when he told me the whole story, I was already sitting in the Cheesecake Factory waiting for Vonnie's late ass.

"Hey, Daddy!"

"Hey, Princess! Why are you so late? You know I'm on the clock, baby."

"I know, I'm sorry, Daddy. I had to meet up with my teacher about the end of the year activities. You know I'll be graduating in a couple of months."

"Yes, I do, and I'm so proud of you, and I know what I'm about to say to you is going to piss you off. But I don't give a damn." By the look she gave me, I knew she didn't like how I said what I'd said.

"I know you mad because I was fighting in the mall, but Eve had it coming."

"I'm going to tell you this one time, and one time only. I want you to dead any type of communication with Bruce's ass. The only reason Eve is coming for you is because you are messing with her baby daddy. If Bruce not still dealing with her, she wouldn't be acting all crazy. Leave him the fuck alone, Vonnie, and I mean it." I was so disappointed when I learned that she had been dealing with Bruce.

"You don't have to worry about that, Daddy. I already got rid of him. I couldn't get past dealing with his ex."

"You better had ended it. I want so much better for you, Princess. I know this is what me and your brother do for a living. But I want you to get you a man with a better plan. You don't have to date a drug dealer. Right now, you don't need to be dating anyone. You need to keep your head in that schoolwork. As for Sy? Leave her the fuck alone too. She ain't no true friend."

Vonnie was sitting there with her lips poked out, but I didn't give a damn. I kept it raw and real with my kids just like my parents did with me.

"Alright, Daddy, I got it. You sound like God-Mami. She told me I don't need no boyfriend and to worry about getting finished with school. She also told me you and Mama only want the best for me. As far as Sy, I haven't been dealing with her, which is why she's pissed off. She's jealous of January."

"Wow, that's crazy. You two have been friends since you were little. I'm shocked, but your mama never liked her. She always said she was jealous of you."

"But why? Whatever I had, I always shared with her."

"This is only the beginning, baby. You ain't seen nothing yet. Sometimes, you can be more of a friend than a person is to you. Friends will come and go, but the real ones will always be around. The scary part is, you don't know who's fake until they reveal themselves," I said, being honest.

Vonnie and I sat and talked for another hour or so while we ate. I assured her we had to do this more. When I was finished, I had shot Bruce a text message to meet up with me. I had to let him know from the rip to stay the fuck away from my baby and keep his hoe away too. Because I ain't have no problem with putting both they asses under the dirt for my princess.

Since the day was slow, I decided to meet up with Bruce as soon as I left the restaurant. He wanted to meet up somewhere, but nope. I popped up right at his crib. I didn't wanna wait for him to come to me. These little niggas be taking too long, and I got shit to do. Once I was out in front of his crib, I saw Eve coming out. All I could do was shake my head. I knew his ass was still fucking with her. Which is why her pill popping ass been coming at my baby. I hurried and hopped out of the car so she could see me. The horrified look on her face caused me to laugh. She hurried and jumped in her car and peeled off.

Once my feet hit the step, Bruce was opening up the door. I didn't even wait for him to tell me to enter. I grabbed him by his neck and pushed him into the house backwards.

"I'mma tell you this one time, and one time only. Stay the fuck away from Vonnie. Make sure you tell your bitch to do the same. Because I don't have no problem with killing a muthafucka over that one." Once I said what I said, I let his neck go.

"Man, D, what the fuck! Your daughter won't even talk to me anymore, so you didn't have to come over here with that bullshit."

"Yes, the fuck I did. I had to make sure you seen my face in person. So, you can see that I ain't playing with ya bitch ass."

"Dalton, don't come to my house acting the fuck like this. If you were someone different, I would have killed your ass by now. Especially since you fired me like that in front of everyone. I thought we were better than that. The only people that should have been fired was Ike and his peeps. You just now put them with me, and you fired me for *your* fuck up. So, yeah, we ain't the best of friends, and if I knew a way with getting away with killing you, I would be all on it."

The way Bruce was talking had me wanting to beat his ass, but I knew shit was too hot out here, and if I killed him, shit would be all fucked up.

"Whatever, lil' nigga! So, what you got going on?" I asked.

"None of your damn business. You said what you wanted to say. Now can you get the hell out of my house?"

"I'm gon' leave before I kill ya ass. The only reason I won't do shit to you is because I know how hot it is, and I don't need that heat, but if I hear you or ya bitch been near my daughter again, all bets are off. And I don't give a fuck where you are or who you with. You gon' have to answer to me."

I hurried and got the fuck up out of his house before I lost it. Once I got to my car and jumped in, I felt like someone was staring at me from across the street. But when I looked up, only parked cars were seen. The feeling was so strong, so I knew it was true. I jumped in my car, then took off, making sure to keep my eye on my surroundings.

TWENTY

When I found out that Vonnie was messing with Bruce, I wanted to beat the shit out of her and him. Vonnie new the fuck better. I knew I did shit I wasn't supposed to do. Which is why I was trying to get this money so I could get my life on a better track. I wanted the best for my sister, and that was what she was going to have. She didn't need no dude like me or our pops.

My phone rung, bringing me out of my thoughts.

"Yo', Boss, meet me at the trap on 32nd! It was just hit!" Quay, one of my workers, yelled in the phone, causing me to jump up.

I hurried and pulled my phone out to call Haas, but the phone went straight to voicemail. He probably was already in route to the trap. This was the first time this shit ever happened to us, and the shit had me pissed the hell off. Who in the hell was messing with me and my business? I hurried and jumped in my whip and made my way to the trap, which was ten minutes away.

After speeding like a crazy person, I parked in the corner store parking lot that was next to the trap. Everybody was standing around, but what really caught my eye was the ambulance. I didn't want to be seen by law enforcement, but I needed to see what the fuck was going on. I pulled out my phone and shot Quay a text, telling him to meet me at the car. Ten minutes later, he walked over to me, but the look on his face let me know something serious happened.

"What the fuck went down?"

"As soon as Haas came to do the pickup, a couple of niggas came in with ski mask on and robbed the place. Haas shot one of the niggas before dude shot back."

The sound of hearing that my right hand had been hit had me fucked up instantly.

"What did you just say?"

"I said Haas was hit. They already took him to the hospital, and his mama is on her way. I already hit Dalton too."

"Which hospital?"

"They rushed him to Cooper Trauma. He was fucked up, Boss."

"Chill out here and wait 'til the cops leave. Once they do, head in and check it out, then lock up. When I leave the hospital, I'mma hit you up, and I want you to gather everyone that was at this trap for a meeting."

"Alright, Boss, I got you," Quay said right before we dapped watch each other up.

I hopped in my whip, then peeled off to make my way to the hospital. On my way, I shot my mama and Vonnie a text, letting them know to meet me at the hospital.

I had to let them know because Haas was our family. Yeah, his mama was living, but he really didn't deal with her like that. But I'm sure she was called because of her being his mama. After speeding to the hospital, I hurried and parked my car, then made my way inside.

"Hello, my brother just came in with a bloodshot wound. His name is Hassan Tucker."

"Where is my son?! Where is my son?!" Haas' loud ass Mama came in the emergency room screaming with her ghetto ass. The crazy part was, he probably hadn't even seen her ass in months.

"Hey, Ms. Tucker. I just asked how he was doing."

"I didn't ask you. I asked the people who work here. Now get the hell out my face. Somebody please tell me where my son is."

"Ma'am I'mma need you to calm down. Your son just went in for emergency surgery. He took a bullet to the chest. Everything is fine. They just needed to get the bullet out and sew him back up."

I walked up to the doctor and shook my head. Hearing that Haas was going to be ok was all I needed to hear. Now I was going to go handle my business. I needed to know who the fuck robbed my trap and how much they took.

"Hey, baby. Are you okay?" my mama asked while tapping my shoulder. Her and Vonnie had just walked in.

I faced my mama, and she pulled me in for a hug. She knew how this shit made me feel. She knew Haas was my brother, and somebody was going to have hell to pay.

"Mama, I'm not okay, but since the doctors said he's going to be fine, I'm a little better. I just can't wait 'til I start getting everything in order so I can leave this street stuff alone. I don't want you ever crying over me being shot."

"You're going to get everything together, baby. I know you will, but when you leave out of here to find out what went down, make sure you be careful and call your dad so he can help you."

"Okay, Mama. Can you and Vonnie stay here 'til he wakes up and tell him I'll be back up?"

"I got you, baby. I love you, and be safe."

After I hugged her, I went and grabbed my sister and pulled her in for a hug. She was crying hard as fuck; I knew she was worried about Haas.

"Shhhh…stop crying, sis. He's going to be okay. Plus, you can't let him see you like this. I need you and Mama to stay here and let him know I'll be back. I have to go handle something."

"Frost, please be safe," my little sister said, causing my heart to smile.

I loved her and my mama with all my heart, and I wouldn't know what to do if something happened to either one of them.

It was the next day, and I was sitting in the hospital room next to Haas' bed. He was sleeping, surgery had gone well, and the doctor just wanted him to stay two more days. The sound of the door opening caught my attention.

"Hello, I'm Officer Slone, and this is my partner, Kelly. We're here to ask Mr. Tucker some questions."

"Well, as you see, Mr. Tucker is sleeping, and he doesn't feel up to answering questions. Maybe you should come back at another time. I'm sure he's on some strong meds, so he wouldn't be able to answer you truthfully."

"Since we can't talk to him, how about you answer some questions for him?"

"Nope, I don't have time to talk to either of you."

I could tell I was pissing him off, but I didn't care. How the fuck you gon' ask me questions, but you don't even know if I was there at the time everything went down? They weren't going to catch me slipping. They both turned to leave out the door, but not before they told me that they would be reaching back to me. The minute they walked out of the door, Haas woke right up. I couldn't do shit but shake my head the way that shit just went down.

"Yo', five O just left out the door. They wanted to ask you questions, but I wouldn't let them wake you up. Then they gon' try to talk to me."

"Yeah, they definitely fishing."

"So, what happened?" I asked.

"Everything happened so damn fast, and it had to be someone that knew the time for me to pick up money and drop off supply."

"Don't worry yourself about any of this. I'm going to handle it. Whoever did this is going to pay."

"Did they find out the name of the dude that shot me?"

"No, not yet, but I have people looking into everything."

"I know you on it, bro, but at the same time, I usually handle a lot of stuff for you. I don't need you out here losing focus because you trying to go kill the person that shot me."

"I'm good, Haas. Don't worry about me."

"Alright, Frost. I'mma leave it alone, but before you got out there trying to paint the city red, make sure you remember about all of our plans. You don't wanna fuck that up. I almost fucked it up myself. I shouldn't have shot back, but I did. Now the police are going to be sniffing around my life. So, it's going to be hard for me to do anything. Have you seen Dalton? Where is he? I thought when shit like this go down, he supposed to help us?"

"I haven't talked to him yet today. I said I was going to go see him today when I left here. Quay reached out to him last night, and him not making it here to see if you were good sets off red flags. But we already know what type of dude my pops is, anyway. So, truthfully, I don't expect anything different."

"Yeah, you right, but this shit crazy. I can't wait 'til we get out of this shit, bro. My life flashed before my eyes, and I'm not feeling this shit at all. I wanna go kill the muthafucka that set all of this up, but then again, I just wanna leave it alone and keep moving to get the fuck out of this shit for real."

A light tap on his room door brought us out of our conversation. We both looked up, and Vonnie was coming in. I knew she would be coming up here today, but I just didn't know what time.

"Hey, y'all!" she said with a huge smile on her face, which brightened my day. Since the last time I saw her last night, she was crying her heart out.

"Hey, sis! What are you doing here?"

"I came to see how Haas is doing. Plus, I brought him something to eat," she said, holding the black corner store bag up.

"Hey, Vonnie, and thanks for the food, ma. I'm hungry, and this food is horrible," Haas said.

I got up and pulled her in for a hug, then kissed her cheek. I then walked back over to the bed and dapped Haas up. I was tired as fuck, and I was going to go ahead and head home to take a nap before I got up to go find Dalton's ass.

"I'm gon' go ahead and head out. I'm tired as hell due to being up all night long."

When I left the hospital last night, Quay had set up a little meeting, and what I found out had me wanting to go the fuck off, but like Haas said, we needed to think smart. What really bothered me was my pops not showing up yet. I needed to talk to his ass, like yesterday. But still haven't talked to him yet. I hated to do it, but I was going to get my mama to reach out. If he didn't answer anyone, I knew he was going to answer to her.

"Alright, bro. Go ahead and get you some rest and be careful. Keep me posted on whatever you find out."

"I got you, bro. Don't even worry about it. Get you some rest today too," I spoke.

"See you later, big head," Vonnie said while giving me another hug.

Once I was finished saying my goodbyes, I headed out the hospital with one plan in mind: to get some fucking sleep. My eyelids were heavy, and as soon as I showered, that was going to be it when I hit the house.

After hopping in my whip and speeding through the city, I made it to my crib in ten minutes, tops. Once I parked, I noticed someone sitting on my step. When I looked up, it was Keet. Which was crazy because I hadn't talked to her since the last time she was here when she left the letter. I wasn't even gon' to lie. I missed her fine ass. Then the thought came to mind how fucking her in the shower and eating some food would put me right out. I noticed her wiping the tears from her eyes when I walked up.

"What's wrong, ma? Why are you crying?"

When she noticed it was me, she jumped up and ran in my arms. "Oh My God! Frost, I thought we lost you!" she said, kind of confusing me.

"What are you talking about, Keet?"

"I'm talking about our baby, Frost. I'm pregnant."

What she had just said caused my breath to leave my body for a second. I used protection what her ass every time. What the fuck she mean, she pregnant?

"How is that even possible?"

"See I knew you weren't going to believe me, which is why I didn't wanna say anything. It's not like we haven't been fucking like crazy since I've been back down here. Yeah, we used condoms, but we've had a couple of busted ones. Don't act like you don't remember."

By the time she was finished with her last statement, the tears fell uncontrollably. I then grabbed her and pulled her close to me. I wasn't ready for no fucking

kids, especially by her, but I was too fucking tired to even

get into this with her right now. I needed food, a shower,

and some fucking sleep. After we pulled a part, I grabbed

her hand, and we walked into the house. My life was

already in an uproar. How the fuck was I going to bring a

baby into this world that I wasn't even ready for?

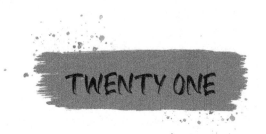

TWENTY ONE

Dalton

Somebody was, indeed, following me, and I had finally found out who it was, but not until I was hit upside my head and placed in the back of a big ass rig truck. I woke up with a bad ass headache, and my hands were chained to the floor. The truck was empty, and I had yet to see who the fuck put me in here. He had to be a bad muthafucka to mess with me. The sound of the truck door opening brought me out of my thoughts. I looked up, and who it was caused my eyes to get big as saucers.

"So, you are finally up," Luther said with a sinister laugh.

"I hope ya stupid ass know what the fuck you are doing."

"Dalton, I've been trying to let you know for years now that I ain't scared of you. You think because you're a big-time dirty cop that you put fear in my heart. I got a better one for you. You should never fuck with a crazy, unstable person. I kept telling Vickie to leave you the fuck alone because she didn't want these problems. Then she thought I was just gon' leave her. I told her ass, hell no. I wasn't giving y'all an open window to get back together. I'll kill her first."

The sound of him saying that caused me to get angry, and I tried to get out of the chains he had me in, but they were tight as fuck. They just caused me to hurt my wrists. I was sure I was going to have a bruise on my shit.

"You not getting the fuck out of them, so stop fucking trying."

"Luther, what do you want, man? If you let me go, I'll leave Vickie alone. I promise you that, and I won't report this. It will be water thrown under the bridge. I promise you that."

"There you go again thinking that you smart, and I'm dumb," Luther said while hitting me in the head with the butt of a gun.

"OUCH! What the fuck?! You know you as good as dead when I get the fuck out of here!" I yelled.

"You may be right. I may end up dead, I may not. It truly depends on your lover and my wife's decision. Now take this phone and text her. Let her know we are meeting at the Crown Plaza in Cherry Hill. Tell her you switched the hotel because I knew where your original spot was. Tell her you're working late, so stay there 'til you get off."

"How will this work? She's not going to stay late because you're in town."

"I'm asking the questions and giving the fucking orders! Just do what the fuck I said! What, you think I'm working on a plan that I didn't sort out first? You must have really thought I was a dumb ass nigga."

"You really will end your life over some pussy?" I asked.

"Would you ruin your life over Vickie?"

I didn't answer. I just looked at him with a mean glare. I could tell he was getting angry because I didn't answer him. Before I knew it, he was delivering another hit to my head.

"Come on, man. You gon' knock me unconscious!"

"Answer the fucking question then!" he yelled.

"Yes, I would do anything for Vickie and my kids."

"Nigga, I didn't ask about them damn kids. I said Vickie, and you answered just the way I knew you would. So, yup, you would do anything for pussy too. Especially Vickie's pussy. I was shocked I would still be craving her pussy like I do, since she's older than my usual candidates. That's the reason why I asked her to marry me because she kept my nose wide open, and she was the only woman my age that was able to keep me from going back into my dark past. Because truth be told, back in my old days, I would have rather had your daughter." He chuckled, causing my blood to boil.

"Muthafucka, if you ever touch my daughter, I will kill you and turn my own self the fuck in!" I said, being truthful.

His laughs were angering me, and I couldn't wait 'til I got the fuck out of these chains. This is one of the prime examples why I told Vickie she should have told me that this cat knew about us. You never know when a person has lost it until it happened.

"Oh, I ain't gon' mess with lil' Vonnie. I'm gon' get my wife back. At least, that's what my plan is, so like I said a minute ago, it's all up to Vickie. See, I know my wife. If you weren't pressuring her, she wouldn't have been dealing with you. So, once I put it all out on the table, I know she gon' go with what I say. After that, then I'll possibly let you go. Then again, it's a lot of people that wouldn't mind your ass being dead. So, maybe they'll take you off my hands."

He was right. It was a lot of people that didn't care for me, but they just let the shit go since I was a cop. A powerful one at that.

"I'll leave your wife alone, man. Just let me go," I pleaded.

The sound of my phone going off got our attention. I couldn't look at it since he had taken it back from me.

"She always text you right back, but when I'm on the road, it takes her hours to text back. She started slipping, which is how I found out she was dipping back. I kept contemplating with myself about taking this damn job. I liked working in the city, but nope. She talked me into taking this job because it doubled my salary. I'm thinking she wanted to better our family, but nope. She wanted me out of town so she can jump on your dick every chance she had."

"Come on, man. Let me loose, and I'll tell her it's over. As a matter of fact, pass me my phone, and I'll tell her we done. I need to get out of here, man. I know people are looking for me."

"You're not getting out of here that fucking easy. People are looking for you, though. There was a shooting and robbery at one of the traps, and Haas got hit. My wife steadily texting you this shit. I guess you should have taught her never to talk like this on the phone. She must don't know phones get tapped all the time." He chuckled while shaking his head.

"I really need to get out of here before my boss starts looking for me."

I tried to convince him I needed to get out of here because of my boss, but I knew I needed to get out of here because I knew Frost was pissed with me. The trap was robbed, Haas was hit, and I was nowhere to be found. This shit didn't look good on my end.

"Don't worry, your boss will be fine. He thinks you on the case. I texted him letting him know you found out some new evidence, and you'll get back to him as soon as you have everything concrete. I told you I thought all of this through before I put the plan in motion. Now let me get out of here. I have to put some other shit in motion before I go meet up with my wife and your mistress."

This dude was really crazy, and I hoped he didn't hurt Vickie or anyone else. He truly was fucked up in the head, and I was now pissed that I wasn't going to be able to get the fuck out of here to save her. I wasn't a praying dude, but that was the only thing I had to do at this moment.

TWENTY TWO

I had a long day between school and work. I was about ready to quit this job, but I liked having my own money. I had money saved up for when I was ready to be on my own. I didn't have anybody to help me, so I needed my own money. I had just got home, and the house was empty. I had no clue where anyone was but Luther and Vonnie. Mama Vickie probably was with Dalton since that's been what she's been doing lately. The boys were with their grandma for the weekend. So, I figured after I eat, I would watch a little TV.

My phone ringing brought me out of my thoughts. When I looked at it, I saw Ms. Lucas' name flash across the screen. I answered right away since it had been a minute since I had talked to her.

"Hello, January! How are you?"

"Hello, Ms. Lucas! I'm great. I was just saying to myself I needed to call you to let you know how I was doing."

"I guess we both were thinking of each other. How's Vickie doing? I've been trying to reach her but haven't been getting any response."

"She's doing great. She just been busy taking care of home. The boys have practice and all types of stuff. She makes sure she keeps them busy, you know?"

"Yeah, that sounds like Vickie. So, how have you gotten adjusted? How's school?"

"I've adjusted well. They treat me like I'm family. As far as school, I'm doing well, considering everything I've been through. I'm graduating top of my class. I also only have to go to school a half-day since my grades are so impeccable. I've just about reached the credits I need to graduate."

"Oh, my goodness, January, that is great to hear! Remember when you finish school, make sure you call me in case you need any help. I'm so proud of you. I've helped so many girls out, but your story is one for the books."

Ms. Lucas caused a big smile to creep up on my face. Although some days are hard for me, on others, I'm so proud of myself because I really have come so far.

"Thanks so much! Hearing that means so much to me. I was wondering if you can send me the information you tried to give me when I was first released? I have so much going for myself, and I'm ready to see a psychologist."

"I'm glad to hear you're ready to talk about your life. I'mma be real with you, January. I had a messed-up childhood similar to yours, and it was like, every time I made it one step forward, I got set back a hundred steps. The road to a better life and success will not be easy, baby. But you got this. You just have to stay strong. You will get tested in every way possible, but you have to come back up swinging."

Hearing that she went through a hard past like me, then to look at her now helping people like me and her, spoke volumes. It made me realize that there is definitely room for a better me and life after the hell I've been through.

"Thank you so much for telling me this, Ms. Lucas. Your words of encouragement are definitely motivation. I know I'm getting a full scholarship to some nice college, and I'm just gon' pack up and go. I will definitely make sure before I go, I give you a call."

"You make sure you do that, and also make sure you give me an invitation for the party because I know Vickie is going to go all out for you and LaVonya."

"Of course, I'll send you an invitation, and thanks so much for reaching out, Ms. Lucas."

"No problem, January, and remember, if you ever need me, my line is always open."

After we disconnected our call, I gathered all of my things to get ready for my shower. I was in such a great mood after that conversation. Once I entered the bathroom, I turned the Bluetooth speaker on and started my playlist that Vonnie sent me. It was mixed with old and new music, and I loved it. I put my hair up in a messy bun, then turned the water to the temperature I liked and hopped in. I danced and smiled while showering.

I stayed in the water until it started to get a little on the cool side. Then I realized it was time for me to get out of the shower. I turned the water off and dried off. Once I was dry, I threw my robe on, then headed to my bedroom. On my way out of the bathroom, I bumped right into Luther.

"Oh, shit! Luther, you scared me. I didn't even know you were here," I said, startled.

I didn't even know my robe had flew open until I followed his eyes down to my breasts. I hurried and closed it, then headed to my room. Right before I closed the door, he licked his lips, then smiled. That was the creepiest shit in the world, and it gave me and uneasy feeling. Right then and there, I was going to get dressed and get my ass up out of here until someone came home.

I threw on a pair of sweats and a t-shirt. Then I put my feet in my Jordan 12's. Once I was completely dressed, I called Vonnie, but she didn't answer. I called

Mama Vickie, and she didn't answer, either. I thought about calling Frost, but I hadn't talked to him since we kissed. I mean, I saw him the day Vonnie and I were fighting at the mall, but he didn't say shit to me. He was basically cursing Vonnie the hell out.

Since I couldn't get in touch with anyone, I decided I would just go out and take a walk to the park or something. Once I had my mind made up, I walked out of my room and downstairs. I decided to go in the kitchen to get me a water. The sound of Luther walking into the kitchen caused me to feel some type of way.

"Hey there, January! Would you happen to know where your Mama Vickie is?"

"No. No one was here when I made it home. When she gets in, tell her I took a walk, please?" I said while heading out of the kitchen 'til he pulled me back.

"I'm not going to tell her anything because you're not going anywhere. I need you to stay here with me and keep me company. Your Mama Vickie is probably with her jump off. I know you know about it. Apparently, everybody knew about it except for me."

"Luther, I don't have no idea what you're talking about," I said in a frightened tone.

"Yes, you do you little bitch!" he said in so much anger while pushing me back in the kitchen.

"Luther, please! I don't know what you're talking about," I cried out once more this time, tears were actually running down my face.

"You don't have to be scared; I'm not gon' hurt you. I actually think we both can benefit from this. It's been a minute since I had some pussy, and it's been a while since anyone's touched that little pussy. That shit's probably tight as fuck. Yeah, I heard about you before you even got here. I fussed with Vickie about bringing a girl here because I knew Frost would be here. But for some reason, Frost been sleeping. I've been watching you since you first came here, and I've been trying to hold myself back, but when your robe flew open, I said, I gotta have it," he said while kissing my neck, making me sick to my stomach. He then lifted me up and sat me on the counter.

I was so scared it caused me to be numb to the point I didn't even feel him pick me up.

"Please, don't hurt me, Luther," I cried.

"I'm not gon' hurt you, baby girl. I'm just gon' make you feel good. You see what you done did to me? You smell so damn good," he said while using his free hand to stroke himself.

My palms were sweaty, my stomach was cramping, and I began to shake. I tried to get up off the counter, and he grabbed me by my throat. The more I tried to move, the more he squeezed. He then grabbed the crouch of my sweats and snatched them forward, causing them to slide right down. He gripped and pulled so hard my panties came down too. Once my bottoms were slid to my knees, he let his dick out of his pants. I had to think fast, or he was going to enter me. I remembered instantly where I was, and it just so happened that his dumb ass placed me on the counter right next to the Keurig machine and the knife Block.

"Luther, can you do something for me right quick?"

"I'll do anything you want me to as long as it's leading to getting some of that sweet, clean pussy."

"I want you to taste it first," I said while vomit formed in my throat.

"I knew you was a little freak, especially after I heard the things your mama had you doing. You probably fuck better than my wife," he said in an excited tone.

As soon as he bent down, and I felt his hot breath on my pussy, I picked up the knife block and hit him right upside the head with it. I then hopped off the counter, pulled my pants up, and ran right out the door.

I didn't have my phone or anything, but I knew we were out in Pennsauken, and Frost was out in Cramer Hill, which wasn't that far away. I ran until I couldn't see the house anymore. I was so fucked up at the moment. I didn't know what the hell to do.

The adrenaline in my body was going crazy, causing me to walk in speed. The tears were running down my face, and at this point in my life, I just wanted to die because it was truly like I couldn't catch a break.

I didn't know how long it took me to walk here, but I knew it was a little while. I was now standing in front of Frost's house. I hurried and walked up the steps, then knocked on the door. Some chick came to the door, and the look on her face showed me that she wasn't happy to see me.

"May I help you?"

"I need to see Frost. It's an emergency."

"Well, he is sleeping, and I'm not waking him up for a bitch that I don't know."

"Look, I need to talk to him about something! I'm his sister!"

"Listen, little girl. I know what Frost sister look like, and I know she ain't you. Plus, I don't do that bro and sis shit. All niggas in the streets got sisters that they be fucking, if his mama ain't birthed you, I ain't trying to hear it. So, miss me with the bullshit. Oh, and make this your last time coming here. Frost and I are about to be parents, and we don't need nobody trying to fuck up what we have," she said right before she closed the door in my face.

Hearing Frost was having a baby had me crushed. I knew we weren't together, nor was we even talking like that. But I knew how I felt about him, and I was so hurt. Feeling defeated and not really wanting to talk to anyone,

I decided to head to the park for some fresh air until I decided what the fuck I was going to do.

I made my way to the park, which was another ten-to-fifteen minute walk. My feet were hurting, and I couldn't wait to sit my ass down on a bench. When I made it, I saw a bunch of dudes in the park. They looked like some of the dudes that were at Frost's party. At first, it bothered me, but then I said fuck it. I needed to rest and get my thoughts in order. I needed to figure out where I was going to stay for the night. Because I knew I wasn't going back to that house.

As soon as I found an empty bench and sat down, it didn't take a nigga long to come over to try and talk to me. But when I looked up and saw who it was, I felt bad, being as though he gave me his number, and I never called him. Maybe I should have since now I know Frost is in a relationship.

"Hey there, pretty lady! I would ask can I have your number, but you ain't gon' call me anyway." He chuckled while shaking his head.

"I'm sorry. I just be busy between work and school. How have you been?"

"I've been good, ma. What are you doing in this park, and it's about to get dark?"

"I just needed to get away right quick. Shit not going good at the crib," I said, making sure not to tell him too much.

"I see. Well, how about you chill with me for a little bit? You don't have to be scared. I know you Frost people, and I'll make sure I keep you safe."

I thought to myself before I answered, but I would probably be safer with him than sitting in a dark ass park. Especially since he knew Frost. One thing I'd learned since I'd been with them was, him and his daddy were powerful people in this city.

"Okay. I guess it won't hurt. Ike, right?" I asked, causing him to smile.

"Oh, so you remembered my name?"

"Yup, and mine is January, in case you didn't remember mine." I smiled.

"Come on, ma, let's go. You hungry?" he asked while we headed to his car.

I didn't know what my life was going to bring after today, and to be honest, I didn't wanna know. I just wanted something to take my mind off the events that happened today.

TWENTY THREE

It had been exactly twenty-four hours since Keet showed up at my crib. We still hadn't really discussed the whole pregnancy thing since my pops was still missing. At first, I was pissed off at him, but now I knew something was going on. I had reported a missing's person report, and I also put my own men on the job.

"Your Godfather is downstairs," Keet said while entering my bedroom.

"Yo', I keep telling you to stop answering my fucking door. You don't live here; you only visiting. If you keep it up, I'm going to kick ya ass out!" I barked.

She sucked her teeth and rolled her eyes. I was sick of her ass, and it was time for her to head out.

I headed downstairs to see what Poppy wanted. I knew he was looking for my pops too. They might not have been on speaking terms, but their bond was everything.

"Hey, Poppy, what's up?" I said while pulling him in for a one-arm hug.

"How are you holding up, son?"

"I'm good. I just wanna make sure my pops is good. Have you heard anything?"

"No, I haven't heard anything about your pops, but I did hear that some of Lucci's men may have hit your trap. I also heard that Bruce and them been over the bridge working for Lucci and his crew."

"You got to be fucking kidding me? I had a feeling it was them niggas, but them working for Lucci is a shock."

"Did you know Lucci is Ike's cousin?"

"You know what? I think Haas mentioned that shit to me. Damn, I didn't pay it no mind back then. So, them niggas hit my trap because they were mad they got fired and Dalton put me up on more traps and more men? The jealous shit be real."

"Yeah, it do. You have to be careful of that shit in this business. I found out that they be staying in this big ass house out in Parkside. It used to be a group home back in the day. Lucci purchased it and let Ike and them stay in it, and them little niggas ain't doing shit but partying and acting wild. Doing some shit to get them caught up. I know they be over the bridge selling they shit. But you know damn well they still probably selling shit on the Southside since Dalton closed them traps down. I got one of my men watching they asses. So, whenever you ready to go over there to talk to them niggas, I'm down."

"Okay, Poppy. Thank you so much. I really appreciate you."

"No thanks needed, son. You know I got you. Now what's going on here? What is that girl doing answering your door?"

I looked at him, signaling him to follow me outside on the front porch. I didn't want Keet to hear what I was saying.

"Man, the day after Haas was shot, she popped up over here, and she told me she's pregnant."

He looked at me, then started shaking his head. "Are you sure it's your baby?"

"I mean, I strapped up, but we had a couple of accidents. The condom broke a couple of times, but Poppy, something telling me she's lying because she tried that 'not moving back home shit and staying with me,' and I told her I wasn't ready for all that. Then she comes back days later talking about she pregnant. I just feel like it's some bullshit."

"If you feel like that deep down inside, then it must be bullshit. But you still have to get a test done because you know the condom broke. If you not into her, you don't have to stay with her because she's pregnant, son. You'll never be happy. You can be a great father while co-parenting."

I had been going back and forth with myself all night worried about how shit would look if I abandoned her and my seed. But Poppy had a point. I didn't have to stay if I didn't wanna be with her. I could still take care and support my kid.

"You're right, and that's exactly what I'm going to tell her. First, I need to go get some pregnancy test and make her take them right in front of me. You know, to make sure she really pregnant. Then, I'll just take it from there."

The minute Poppy was about to speak, my phone started ringing, bringing us out of our conversation. I saw it was Vonnie, and I picked right up.

"Frost, nobody came home last night, and I'm scared. I even found January's phone on her bed in her room."

"What you mean?"

"When I came in from visiting Haas, nobody was home. I just thought they went out, so I didn't think anything of it. I just went in my room and went to bed."

"Is Luther on the road?"

"Yes. He been on the road since the beginning of the week. At first, I thought Mama could be with Daddy, but he was missing, while mama and me was together yesterday. Frost, please find them."

"Okay, baby girl. I'mma figure out what's up. I need you to go over Poppy house and chill with Mami Tisha until I let you know it's ok to go home. Text me when you get there."

"Okay, Frost, I love you, and please be safe."

"Shit just got real, and I tell you this much. Nothing better not had happened to my mama behind Dalton's shit, Poppy."

"What's going on?"

"Vonnie said my mama didn't come home. Usually, she with Dalton, but he been missing for a couple days already. So, where the fuck is my mama, Poppy?" I snapped.

"I don't know what the fuck is going on, but we going to get down to the bottom of this shit. Go throw some clothes on. I'm about to call some of my boys, and we gon' go over to that spot to talk to them niggas and see if they heard anything about Dalton. I'm sure once we find him, we will find your mama."

"It's not just my Mama. Vonnie said January didn't come home, either, and because of what she been through, I know she just didn't hang out all night."

I really felt some type of way about this shit, and I needed everybody found and back home safe.

We had been chilling out front for a little over a half-hour, and I was ready to go in. Poppy made sure everybody was in place. Once we did that, Poppy and I walked right up to the front door. I placed my gun right at the side of the dude's head that was smoking and sitting on the front patio step.

"Who the fuck is in there?"

"Snoop and Ike are in the back room with this bitch. Everybody else just ran to Wawa."

"Get the fuck up and come on!" Poppy snapped, making the dude get up while I made my way into the house.

Since he said the room was in the back of the house, I made my way back there. All I heard was yelling.

"Bitch, you been here all night on the shy shit. You gon' have to come off that pussy, or you can get the fuck out!" I heard Ike yelling while Snoop was laughing.

"You said you weren't going to hurt me. I thought you said you were Frost's friend?" The sound of January's voice could be heard.

I was in a daze until I heard what sounded like a smack. I then kicked the door in, and it was, indeed, January sitting on the bed holding her face, while Ike was on top of her.

"Nigga, get the fuck off her!" I yelled while snatching Ike's stupid ass up.

I could see Snoop jumping up from the corner if my eye. I hurried and shot that nigga, causing him to fall to the floor. Two of Poppy's men came running in the room.

"Take them assholes and put them in the trunk. We going to the spot to have a talk."

After they took them out of the room, I walked over to January to try to help her up. But she snatched away from me.

"Miss J, what the fuck is wrong with you coming over here with these guys? You don't even know them, ma. What if I didn't show up?"

"Like you really care about me."

"Don't talk like that, ma. Now, come on. We don't have time for this. I need to get you home. I have business to take care of."

Her eyes grew big, and she looked frightened. From the way she was looking, I knew something was wrong.

"I'm not going there. I can't go there. I'm not safe there," she cried out while the tears rolled down her face.

"Miss J, what's wrong, baby girl? Did something happen to you."

"He tried to rape me, and you weren't there. You said you would keep me safe. You said you would make sure I was good. But when I got to your house, your baby mama let me know loud and clear that I didn't need to show up there ever again. You weren't around to keep me safe like you said. He tried to rape me!" January said once more before I took her in my arms.

"Come on, son. We have to get the fuck out of here, NOW!" Poppy yelled while walking up behind us.

"January, who tried to rape you, ma?"

"L-L-L-Luther did."

Talk about complete shock. I couldn't believe what the fuck she just told me. But I knew Luther was newly added to my list of people that were about to feel my rage.

To stay updated with Tyanna and Tyanna Presents please join my reading group...

Made in the USA
Monee, IL
25 May 2021